WT
14.99

JAN 0 7

The Return of the Cupcaked Crusader...

Horace reached into his backpack, took out his Cupcaked Crusader costume, and pulled it over his clothes. It had a large collar that stood up around Horace's ears with a cape attached, and a wing under each arm. The purple taffeta costume covered Horace from head to toe and fingertip to fingertip.

As Horace slipped his hands into the gloves of the costume, he felt the skin on his fingers grow tighter and tighter. He looked down in amazement as large pieces of steel suddenly cut through the costume. His fingernails had become six-inch-long steel scoops!

Cupcaked-Crusader-Incredible!

For Jonathan David,
my older brother, whom I once pushed out the front door of the house when he had no clothes on when he was nine and I was seven and then I locked the door and he ran around the yard naked. (Don't try this or you might get punished by your mom or dad like I was.)

—L.D.

Horace Splattly

THE CUPCAKED CRUSADER

When Second Graders Attack

by Lawrence David

illustrated by Barry Gott

PUFFIN BOOKS

PUFFIN BOOKS
Published by the Penguin Group
Penguin Putnam Books for Young Readers,
345 Hudson Street, New York, New York 10014, U.S.A.
Penguin Books Ltd, 80 Strand, London WC2R ORL, England
Penguin Books Australia Ltd, Ringwood, Victoria, Australia
Penguin Books Canada Ltd, 10 Alcorn Avenue, Toronto, Ontario, Canada M4V 3B2
Penguin Books (N.Z.) Ltd, 182-190 Wairau Road, Auckland 10, New Zealand

Penguin Books Ltd, Registered Offices: Harmondsworth, Middlesex, England

Published simultaneously by Dutton Children's Books and Puffin Books,
divisions of Penguin Putnam Books for Young Readers, 2002

5 7 9 10 8 6

Copyright © Lawrence David, 2002
Illustrations copyright © Barry Gott, 2002
All rights reserved.

Puffin ISBN 0-14-230118-3

Printed in the United States of America

Contents

HORACE IS A LITTLE TEAPOT

Horace Splattly and the Blootin twins stood outside Blootinville Elementary at the end of another school day. Kids scattered across the school yard, laughing, hopping on their skateboards, and running for their buses to take them home.

Horace looked at his two friends. "Do you have *The Splattly and Blootin Big Notebook of Worldwide Conspiracies?*" he asked.

Xax (rhymes with "tacks") Blootin shook his long blond bangs over his face and patted his backpack. "Sure do."

Auggie (rhymes with "foggy") Blootin brushed his long blond bangs across the top of his head.

"Do we have to wait for your sister?" he asked.

Horace shook his head and smiled. "Nope, Melody has one of her Lily Deaver Scout meetings. Let's jet to my house."

"Help! Oh, please please help!"

Horace's ears perked up. It sounded as if a girl was calling from the back of the school, where workers had dug a big pit for the school's new Snailtorium. It was going to be a place where kids could bring their pet snails to special snail concerts, snail movies, and snail plays.

"Help! Oh me—oh my!"

Horace knew that voice. It belonged to Sara Willow, the prettiest girl in all of Blootinville. Nothing made Horace happier than when they played dodgeball in P.E., and Sara chose to throw that big red rubber ball at him. She'd toss it as hard as she could and knock Horace to the ground. And Horace didn't care. To Horace, being hit with Sara's ball was just the same as if she kissed him, only without all the yucky germs and spit.

But off the dodgeball court, Sara didn't seem to realize that Horace existed. The biggest problem Horace had in getting Sara to talk to him was that he was the shortest kid in Blootinville Elementary except for the kindergartners and six of the first graders. He was so short that when Ms. Sparkles, his English teacher, asked him to be the Christmas tree in the winter pageant, she had to make him a stump instead.

"Help!" Sara screamed at the top of her pretty lungs.

And now Sara needed his help.

Horace grabbed Xax and Auggie, pulling them behind a row of bushes and tossing his backpack to the ground.

"What's going on?" Auggie asked.

Horace unzipped a pocket of his backpack and pulled out a small aluminum-foil ball. "Didn't you hear that?" he asked.

"Hear what?" Xax replied. He'd been too busy counting the ants crawling on the sidewalk to pay attention. Xax counted things the way other people breathed—it was his favorite hobby.

"Help! Oh dear, please help!"

"*That*," Horace said.

Other kids had heard it, too, and were hurrying across the playground to see what was happening.

Horace looked at the twins. "It's Sara Willow. She needs me to save her from something dangerous." He unwrapped the aluminum ball and displayed a cupcake. It was gray with crumbly, spotted pebble things on top.

"Is that one of Melody's cupcakes?" Auggie asked.

Without answering, Horace broke the cupcake in two and stuffed one half in his mouth. He began chewing. It tasted completely grimy, like he was eating the ashes from the bottom of the Splattlys' backyard barbecue.

"Do you know what it might do to you?" Xax asked, his voice trembling with fear. "I know they give you superpowers, but don't they also do weird things to you before the superpowers come?" He looked at the ground and began counting blades of grass to calm his nerves.

Auggie nodded, agreeing with his brother. "Remember how you ate that white one and then you couldn't move at all?" he asked. "What if that happens? Didn't your sister tell you never to eat them without her around in case something goes wrong?"

Horace rewrapped the remaining half and put it in his backpack. "I don't care what she said. She just wants to be in charge all the time. I mean, think about it: Should a superhero have to ask his little sister for permission to save someone?" he declared. He glanced around. "Uh, remember to always pretend you don't know that the Cupcaked Crusader is really me. If Melody finds out I told you, she might stop making the cupcakes." He reached into the bottom of his backpack. "Now I'll just put on my Cupcaked Crusader costume and save Sara. That's just—"

But before Horace could finish his sentence, his face froze. He stopped talking, shut his eyes, and began rolling his head in circles. "I'm a little teapot, short and stout," he sang loudly in a sweet, girly voice. "Here is my handle, here is my spout."

"Horace, are you okay?" Auggie asked.

Horace lifted one arm to be a handle, the other to be a spout, and leaned over to pour tea. "When I get my steam up, I will shout. Tip me over and pour me out."

Xax burst out laughing. "Somehow I don't think Horace pretending to be a teapot is going to save Sara Willow."

Auggie frowned. "This is serious, Xax. What if he can't come out of it?"

"I'm a little teapot, short and stout," Horace began again.

"Who's singing like that?" a girl asked.

Auggie and Xax looked up to find themselves facing the entire second-grade pack of the Lily Deaver troop. Standing at the front of the pack was Melody Splattly, Horace's eight-year-old sister. She may have been two years younger

than Horace, but she was also seven inches taller. Melody stared down at her brother with a curious expression.

The scouts held their lavender Lily Deaver tote bags to their sides. Their lavender Lily Deaver backpacks hung over their shoulders, and each wore matching lavender Lily Deaver shoes, berets, sashes, hair bands, gloves, and opera glasses around their necks.

"I'm a little teapot, short and stout," Horace sang.

Melody laughed, and her dark brown hair gently bounced around her head. "What's the matter with him?" she asked. "He looks crazier than a boy in a pair of Lily Deaver high-heel cooking clogs."

Xax and Auggie looked at each other, then back to the twenty pairs of Lily Deaver scout eyes that were staring at them.

THE SECRET OF THE CUPCAKES

The cupcakes were Melody's creation.

She had become a Lily Deaver scout at the age of three and ever since had been devoted to cooking, sewing, dressing, and decorating the Lily Deaver Way. She had a lavender Lily Deaver Cook & Bake Oven, a lavender Lily Deaver Stitch & Thread Sewing Machine, a lavender Lily Deaver Spill & Brew Science Laboratory, and a lavender Lily Deaver lab coat, rubber gloves, spatula, and measuring-spoon set with built-in video cameras so she could record all her experiments from the point of view of the ingredients.

Melody even downloaded recipes off the Lily Deaver website and made the Splattlys' dinner every night. Yesterday she had served Chocolate Chip Chicken and mashed celernips with banana slices.

And what was Melody's greatest concoction? The cupcakes!

A couple of weeks ago, Melody had made four of the treats and threatened to beat her brother up unless he ate them. They looked so disgusting that at first Horace had been afraid to take even one bite, but after his sister cried her eyes out, he finally agreed to try two halves from two different cupcakes. Minutes later, he had the power to fly and to breathe fire. Horace couldn't believe it! He'd become a superhero! Of course his sister had her own ideas. She handed him a purple costume and told him he'd be the Cupcaked Crusader. She even ordered him not to tell anyone about the cupcakes because then Mom and Dad would take away all the things she needed to make the special desserts.

"You're *my* superhero," she told Horace. "Because I'm the one with the cupcakes and recipes. The powers don't last very long, squirt. If you want to keep them, you're going to have to do whatever I say."

But Horace wasn't going to be her servant. Instead of doing whatever his sister said, he had flown all over town and helped people get out of trouble. He'd even flown over to Auggie and Xax's house and told the twins the secret of the cupcakes. By the end of that day, everyone in town knew about the Cupcaked Crusader, but only the Blootin twins and Melody knew he was Horace.

Melody understood that Horace wasn't following *all* her orders, but what she didn't know was that Horace had taken the leftover cupcakes from her room and hid them behind a secret wall panel in his bedroom. And she'd never found out that he'd told the Blootin twins about his secret identity.

Now Horace had tried half a cupcake without

her permission. What were the results? Horace was standing before the entire second-grade Lily Deaver troop singing "I'm a Little Teapot."

• • •

"Here is my handle, here is my spout," Horace sang, rolling his head, keeping his eyes shut.

The Lily Deaver girls began to giggle. Melody took a step toward her brother, lifted her opera glasses to her eyes, and examined his face. "There's something dreadfully wrong with this specimen." She leaned into his ear. "Horace! Horace!" she yelled. When he didn't react, she squinted at the Blootins, suspiciously. "Hmm . . ." She peered at Horace's face and poked his nose with a finger. "Horace, if you don't stop this very instant, when I get home tonight I'll make you take a bath in my new skin-wrinkling raspberry-beet puree." She turned to the Lily Deaver girls. "I made it last night. It wrinkles and colors your skin so you look like a purple rhinoceros. Of course, since Horace is so little, he'll only look like a raisin."

The Lily Deaver girls laughed.

"When I get my steam up, then I will shout," Horace sang.

Auggie and Xax frowned.

Melody shook her head. "My brother has a brain the size of a tadpole."

"Help! Help!" Sara Willow called from the back of the school.

Melody turned around and joined the other Lily Deaver girls. "Come along, girls. Obviously there's no help we can give my *little* brother. Let's go see what's going on behind the school."

The group of girls turned and walked across the school yard to the construction site.

Horace began singing the song again.

"Shut up!" Auggie called in one ear.

"Stop it!" Xax called in the other.

Horace rolled his head and did a little spin. "Tip me over and pour me out," and then he tipped right over and collapsed on the ground.

Chapter 3

SAVING SARA WILLOW

Horace lay in the dirt.

Auggie and Xax shook him lightly.

"Hey, Horace, are you all right?" Auggie asked.

"Do you think he's dead?" Xax asked.

Horace lifted his head and opened his eyes. "Huh? What? No, of course I'm not dead." He sat up and looked around the school yard. "Those cupcakes always make me do something strange before the powers happen. I guess that one makes me sing that song. I hope Melody won't really turn me into a raisin."

"You could hear us the whole time?" Auggie asked.

Horace nodded. "Yup, but the cupcake's powers wouldn't let me talk or do anything. It had complete control over me."

"Pretty creepy," Auggie said.

"So what are your powers?" Xax asked. "Do you feel anything?"

"Won't someone please help me!" Sara Willow called.

Horace shrugged at Xax. "I'm not sure yet, but I hope they happen soon." He reached into his backpack, took out his Cupcaked Crusader costume, and pulled it over his clothes. It had a large collar that stood up around Horace's ears with a cape attached, and a wing under each arm. The purple taffeta costume covered Horace from head to toe and fingertip to fingertip.

As Horace slipped his hands into the gloves of the costume, he felt the skin on his fingers grow tighter and tighter. He looked down in amazement as large pieces of steel suddenly cut through the costume. His fingernails had become six-inch-long steel scoops!

Cupcaked-Crusader-Incredible!

Auggie and Xax gasped.

Horace held up his two hands. It was like having two sets of super-strong gardening tools attached to his body. He smiled at the Blootins. "I guess I just figured out my new superpower," he said with a laugh, and he ran across the playground to the construction site.

• • •

A tall chain-link fence surrounded the site where the Emailtorium was being dug. Horace pushed his way through the crowd. One hundred feet below at the bottom of the pit sat Sara Willow in a pile of dirt. She wore a puffy white shirt and a pretty pink skirt smudged with mud. Her hair swooped over her head like a tornado and was tied with dozens of pink bows. Sara never wore her hair the same way twice.

Sara looked up to see Horace in his disguise. "The Cupcaked Crusader is here to save me! Thank you, thank you!" she called.

"How did you get down there?" Horace asked

in a low tone so that no one would recognize his voice.

Sara hung her head sadly. "The wind blew one of my pretty bows off, and so I climbed over the fence to get it. Now I can't get out," she explained.

"Don't worry," Horace said in his superhero voice. "I'll be there in a minute."

He knelt on the ground and dug with his shovel fingernails into the dirt. The claws were so sharp, they tore through the ground as if it were paper. He quickly tunneled under the fence, digging a path deep underground and breaking through into the bottom of the pit where Sara sat.

All the kids cheered. Principal Nosair stood by the fence clapping his hands. "Hooray for the Cupcaked Crusader! He's always here to save the day!"

Horace slid out of the hole and smiled at Sara. "Ready to climb up through the tunnel and go home?" he asked.

Sara wrinkled her nose. "Do I have to? My hair will get dirty. Can't you just fly me over the fence?"

Horace wrinkled his brow and kicked a foot at the ground. How could he tell her that he didn't have the power to fly today? "Uh, I, uh, forgot my flying license, sorry," he told Sara. "I'm afraid you'll have to crawl through the tunnel, miss."

Sara patted a hand to her hairdo. "Oh, I hate when my hair gets mussed." And with that, she knelt down and began crawling up to the school yard.

• • •

Ten minutes later, after Principal Nosair had thanked the Cupcaked Crusader and gone back into the school, and the other kids had gone home for the day, Sara Willow approached the superhero who had saved her. "I wish you could come to my house for an afternoon snack, Mr. Cupcaked Crusader," she told him. "I think you're really, really cute. But unfortunately, now that my hair's dirty, I have to wash and curl it this afternoon." She gave Horace a little wave. "Thanks for helping me." She ran to catch her bus.

Horace joined Xax and Auggie behind the bushes where they waited with his backpack. "Block me, guys," he asked.

Xax and Auggie stood in front of Horace as he took off his Cupcaked Crusader costume.

Horace peeled off the outfit and tucked it in his backpack. "Did you hear what Sara said?" he asked. "She thinks I'm cute."

Auggie shook his head. "She liked the Cupcaked Crusader, not you, Horace."

Horace stared at his long shovel fingernails and frowned. "Yeah, I guess you're right, but still maybe one day she'll like me."

Xax carefully touched one of Horace's shovel fingernails. "How long do you think these will last? Aren't you afraid they won't go away?"

Horace hid his hands under his backpack so no other kids would see them. Whenever he rubbed his fingers together, they clanged like locker doors. "I hope not for very long. They're kind of heavy."

"So, I guess you're done being a teapot, huh?"

The three boys were startled to see Melody Splattly glaring at her brother. Her arms were folded across her chest, and she pointed her nose in the air. "Xax and Auggie, will you please excuse us. I need to speak to my brother alone."

Horace looked at the twins nervously and clutched his hands together under his backpack so Melody wouldn't see them. "Auggie and Xax are coming to our house this afternoon. They don't have to go away."

Melody turned her back to the Blootins and hissed at Horace, "I know exactly what's going on, so don't think you're so smart. You took my extra cupcakes and now you're playing super-hero whenever you want. The cupcakes aren't toys, Horace. You shouldn't eat them without my supervision. If you eat too much, the powers could mutate and—"

"Stop whining," Horace said, backing away from his sister. "Everything turned out fine. I saved Sara Willow from the pit."

Melody wrinkled her nose. "Maybe so, but that doesn't mean something bad won't happen next time." She tapped a finger to her brother's chest. "And you better not tell Auggie and Xax."

Blip-blip-blippety-blip, a cell phone rang.

Xax took his cell phone out of his pocket. "Not me."

Blip-blip. Blippety-blip-blip.

Auggie took his cell phone out of his pocket. "Not me."

Blip-blip. Blippety-blip-blip.

Melody took a cell phone out of the pocket of her Lily Deaver uniform. "It's me!" she cried, flipping it open. She put the phone to her head. A very serious expression crossed her face, and she spoke in a strange, robotlike voice. "Lily Deaver Scout number zero-one-two-zero-six-three reporting. Yes, sir. I will be there immediately, sir. Yes, sir." She pushed a button, then closed the phone.

"When did you get a cell phone?" Horace asked. "I thought Mom and Dad wouldn't buy you one."

Melody proudly held up the phone. "I don't have to answer your questions. I have a mission to accomplish for Chef Nibbles. He's our new second-grade pack leader. Last week when we had our meeting at his factory, he gave a cell phone to everyone in our troop and fed each of us a bowl of his Famous Canned and Cold

Rotten Tomato Snoodle soup. We're having another meeting today." She slung her lavender Lily Deaver knapsack off her shoulder and held it out to her brother. "Now take this home so I don't have to carry it. Okay?"

Horace didn't reach for the knapsack. He just clutched his hands with the shovel fingernails tighter under his backpack.

Melody looked down at Horace's knapsack then up to his eyes. "Are your hands a little tired?" she asked. She raised her eyebrows. "Well, then I guess we'll just have to do it this way." She lifted the strap of her backpack, hung it over her brother's head, then turned and walked back across the yard to join the other Lily Deaver girls. Each held a bright orange Chef Nibbles phone to her head.

Horace scowled at the backpack around his neck and looked at his friends. "Come on, let's go," he said.

Auggie gave his friend a pat on the shoulder. "At least with Melody busy, we'll be able to hang without her around," he said.

"Yeah, no pesky sister bothering us," Xax said.

Horace nodded. "Yeah, that's true." As he led the boys home, his hands began to shake.

Sfffttt, sfffttt, sfffttt, sfffttt, sfffttt. And as quickly as the shovel fingernails had appeared, they were gone.

Chapter 4

CUPCAKES AND PRICKLES

The boys lay on the floor of Horace's room eating Cheese Celerippos, the most popular snack in Blootinville. They also drank bottles of celernip soda, the most popular drink in all of Blootinville. Celernip was a vegetable that was half celery and half turnip. Blootinville farmers were the only ones in the world who knew how to grow it.

Xax stared hard at a Celerippo laying on his palm.

"What are you doing?" Horace asked.

"Counting all the specks of cheese on my Celerippo," Xax explained. "So far I've counted two hundred and thirty-nine."

Auggie plucked the Celerippo from Xax's hand, stuck it in his mouth, and swallowed.

"Hey!" Xax cried.

Auggie smirked. "Last night when we were watching TV, Xax was so busy counting the sprinkles on his ice cream that he left *The Splattly and Blootin Big Notebook of Worldwide Conspiracies* open on the floor. If I hadn't kicked it under the couch, Dad would have seen it for sure."

Horace gasped. Mayor A. X. Blootin didn't like his sons getting into trouble, and most parents would definitely think investigating the things in *The Splattly and Blootin Big Notebook of Worldwide Conspiracies* would lead their kids to big, big trouble. Whenever the boys saw something or even *thought* anything suspicious might be happening in Blootinville, or the United States, or anywhere or earth, they entered it into their notebook for further investigation. They were certain that any of the weird things in their book could mean disaster for the school, the town, or even the whole wide world. Only they were smart enough to know what was going on—no one else was paying any attention to all this weird stuff.

So far, Xax, Auggie, and Horace had gotten into trouble twice. The first time was when they interrogated Myrna Breckstein in the janitor's closet because they thought she was really an adult pretending to be a ten-year-old kid. The boys found out she wasn't a grown-up, but as punishment they had to clean the boys' bathroom for two weeks.

The second time they got into trouble was when the boys dressed up like fish in order to find out if Mr. Howlly the doughnut maker was really a walrus. The boys were flopping around on the doughnut shop floor, waiting to see if Mr. Howlly would try to eat them when the twins' father walked in. Mayor Blootin got so angry with the boys that he said they could never go into the doughnut shop again.

The question of whether Mr. Howlly was a

walrus or not was still open. The boys were thinking of casting fishing poles with bait on the ends into the window of the shop (to see if they caught Mr. Howlly on a hook or not).

• • •

Auggie took another handful of Celerippos from the bag. "I don't know why you have to count so much," he told his brother.

Xax reached into his backpack and took out the notebook. "There's so much to count, how can I not?" he replied.

Horace took the book from Xax and opened it across the floor. The three boys read the large page before them; on it was the list of conspiracies.

"Will your dad be checking on us soon?" Auggie asked.

Horace looked at the clock. "I don't think so. We should have about fifty minutes until he stops by."

Dr. Hinkle Splattly was a psychiatrist who had an office attached to the Splattly home.

After school, he checked on Horace and Melody between appointments with his patients. Horace and his sister usually had plenty of time to get into and out of trouble before their father looked in on them. And Horace's mom, Mari Splattly, wasn't usually home until seven o'clock. She worked as the publisher of the town newspaper.

"So what should we investigate?" Horace asked, scanning the list. "Do we try to find out more about Mr. Wallingford's Swahili-speaking tulip, or do we spy on Dr. Sylvia Lingmill for proof that she really glues rubber bands to her body and rolls around on the floor doing somersaults?"

Xax pointed a finger at the book. "Can't we investigate whether Tammy Biddy and Cleo Bumratt are really third-grade alien princesses sent here to shelter them from the war that's happening on their own planet?"

Auggie sat up. "I heard that our next-door neighbor Mrs. Dirkwaddle baked Mr. Dirkwaddle in a crunchy peanut-butter cookie and fed him to the elephants in the Blootinville Wild Safari and Car Repair Salon."

Horace handed Auggie a pen. "Write it in the book so we don't forget it," he told him.

"So where should we start?" Xax asked.

"Hold on, I have an idea," Horace replied. He slid under his bed and removed a secret panel from the wall. The best thing about being so small was that no one else could fit under his bed and get to the wood board.

He reached into the wall, took out a ball of aluminum foil, then grabbed his backpack to take out what was left of the cupcake he'd eaten earlier that afternoon. He opened the two packages and set them down on the notebook. "You guys can try cupcakes with me for the first time. Won't that be great?" he asked. "Today we can all be superheroes and solve lots of stuff."

The twins put down their sodas and snack and fixed their eyes on the three half cupcakes and one whole cupcake.

"Don't these cupcakes ever get stale?" Xax asked. "These are over two weeks old, and they look as good as new."

Horace poked one with a finger. "All the special ingredients Melody uses must keep them fresh a lot longer," he explained.

Auggie pointed to the half cupcake that was black and oozing bright orange jelly. "Ew," he said. "Is that the one that made you feel like you were burning up?"

Horace nodded. "At first, but then I could breathe fire," he answered.

Xax bit his lip. "I don't want to feel like I'm burning up." He pointed to the half cupcake with the white spikes on top. "What did that one do?"

Horace held up his arms like an airplane and smiled. "That's the one that let me fly all over Blootinville."

"But how did it make you feel when you ate it?" Auggie asked suspiciously.

Horace dropped his arms. "It made spiky things slither through my body so I couldn't move," he admitted.

"I don't want that to happen to me," Xax said.

Auggie nodded in agreement and pointed to the gray cupcake. "And we saw what that one did."

"I don't want to sing 'I'm a Little Teapot,'" Xax said, shaking his bangs over his eyes. "No way."

Horace frowned and picked the three half cupcakes off the book. "Don't you want to have powers so we can all be superheroes together?"

Auggie and Xax looked at the cupcakes then to each other.

"I don't know, Horace," Auggie said. "They're pretty dangerous."

"You never would have tried them if your sister didn't force you," Xax said.

Horace placed the cupcakes in Xax's open palms. "C'mon, it'll be fun."

Xax looked at Auggie. Auggie looked at Xax. They both looked at the cupcakes.

"Y-you can choose first," Xax told his brother. His hands trembled as he held the cupcakes.

"Uh, why don't you choose first?" Auggie asked. "I mean, I was born four minutes before you, so maybe you should be first now."

Xax held the cupcakes out to his brother. "But that means you're older and smarter."

"Four minutes isn't *much* smarter." Auggie pushed Xax's hands away.

"Won't one of you choose?" Horace asked.

"I think you're afraid," Auggie challenged.

"You're more afraid," Xax accused. "If you're not, then take one." He shoved them under his brother's nose.

"Get those away from me!" Auggie yelled. He smacked Xax's hands, and the three half cupcakes flew out of his brother's grasp, across the room, and out the open bedroom window.

"What's the matter with you guys?!" Horace asked. He ran to the window and peered down. "Yowee-zowee-zooks!" he cried. He raced downstairs and into the backyard, followed quickly by Auggie and Xax.

"Horace, what's the matter?" Auggie asked.

"We'll get them back," Xax promised. "A little dirt won't hurt them."

The three boys stood outside. Horace pointed to a small black porcupine in the middle of the lawn.

"Isn't that your neighbor's pet?" Auggie asked.

"What happened to the cupcakes?" Xax asked.

Horace stomped a foot on the ground. "He's one of Old Man and Old Lady Honker's nine pet porcupines," he explained. "They're raising them to race at the Blootinville Porcupine Racetrack. I think Prickles ate the cupcakes."

"All three?" Auggie asked.

"You still have a whole one more," Xax said.

"Yeah, but what do you think the cupcakes will do to him?" Horace asked.

As if in answer to the question, Prickles raised his head, shut his eyes, and began making squeaky noises. "Eeeka-weaka-teapeet."

"What's he doing?" Xax asked.

Horace stared at the singing porcupine. "I think he's trying to sing 'I'm a Little Teapot,'" he answered.

Auggie burst out in laughter. "And he sings it just about as good as you did."

Horace swatted Auggie with a hand. "I sang it much better than a porcupine!"

Auggie shook his head. "Did not."

Horace stared at the porcupine. "How does he even know that song?" he asked.

Prickles stopped singing the song and thumped his paws to the ground. A blast of smoke burst from his nose, a flame of fire blew from his mouth, and the porcupine scampered from the yard.

"Get him!" Horace called.

The three boys chased after the porcupine, but by the time they got to the front yard, he was nowhere to be found. All they saw was a small hole in the middle of the lawn with smoke billowing out of the opening.

"I didn't think porcupines dug or crawled in holes," Auggie said.

"Or breathed fire," Xax added.

"Most porcupines don't have superpowers," Horace explained. "I wonder if he'll start to fly."

"Shouldn't you crawl in after him?" Xax asked his brother.

"Why me?" Auggie asked.

"You threw the cupcakes out the window."

Auggie glared at his brother. "No, I didn't! You were the one who—"

Suddenly the sound of an explosion filled the air. The twins stopped their arguing and looked down from the Splattlys' yard high atop Hip Hop Toad to the valley of Blootinville below. A large cloud rose from the corner of the shopping center on Main Street where the All-You-Can-Eat Hot Dog Hut was supposed to be. When the cloud lifted, the hot-dog stand was no longer there. In its place was a tower of hot dogs one hundred feet high.

"Wh-what happened to the Hot Dog Hut?" Xax asked nervously as he began counting Horace's eyelashes. "D-d-do you think that Prickles could have dug there that fast?"

"I don't know," Horace replied. "But I think this is a case for the Cupcaked Crusader. Come on, guys, it's time for this fourth-grade super-hero to have an extra-special afterschool snack."

Chapter 5

THE WRIGGLING
BLACK WORM CUPCAKE

Horace dashed to his room and examined the last cupcake on the open notebook. "Eating *all* of one cupcake might give me more special powers," he said.

"But you've never eaten all of one before," Xax told his friend fearfully. "You don't even know what it might do to you."

"My sister wouldn't bake anything that would kill me," he answered. "The other ones worked without hurting me too much. Don't you want to find out if Prickles caused that hot-dog explosion?"

"I don't know, Horace," Auggie said. "Maybe we should just write about the Hot Dog Hut in the notebook."

Horace looked at his friends. "What if some-one needs the Cupcaked Crusader's help? What if there are clues there now that will be gone tomorrow?" He gazed at the cupcake. "Something has to be done this very minute," he told them.

The cupcake sat on the wrinkled aluminum foil in the middle of the notebook. It was made of swirling black and brown cake with chocolate icing. The icing looked delicious, but when the boys examined it closely, they could see it was really a pile of thousands of tiny, wriggling black crawly things.

"It does kind of look scary, doesn't it?" Horace asked.

The twins stuck their tongues out. "Blech," they moaned.

Horace looked out the window at the tower of hot dogs. A superhero had to do many risky things in order to help people. And if eating a scary cupcake was one of the risks Horace had to take, then so be it!

He turned from the window, picked up the

cupcake, and shoved the entire thing into his mouth.

Horace's cheeks bulged. His eyes watered. Inside his mouth, the cupcake began transforming. He could feel the tiny crawly creatures slither off the cake and crawl over his gums and down the back of his throat. But they weren't slimy like worms. They felt kind of furry like caterpillars. And the other weird thing was that the bottom of the cupcake collapsed to the floor of his mouth as if it were a popped balloon. When Horace tried to swallow it, the flattened cupcake wrapped around and covered his tongue like a sock.

Auggie and Xax stared at their friend.

"Are you all right?" Auggie asked.

"Do you feel anything happening?" Xax asked.

Horace could feel the cupcake sock grow tighter around his tongue. He could feel the tiny crawlers wriggling across his gums and tickling his throat. "Mmmt-srrrrr-tsgngn," he replied.

He walked to the mirror on the back of his bedroom door and opened his mouth wide.

Inside his mouth, thousands of tiny caterpillars were spinning thousands of tiny cocoons. Horace wanted to scream, but his mouth was so packed with cocoons and his tongue was bound so tightly that he couldn't utter a sound. Then he felt something thin and slippery inside his mouth, like a piece of thread or a strand of hair. He turned around so his friends could see. When he opened his mouth, a thread slipped past his lips. It was black and shiny and kept growing and growing, first a few inches, then a whole foot.

Xax backed away from Horace. "S-something's growing out of you, buddy."

"W-what should we do?" Auggie asked.

Horace was frozen with fear. The thread grew longer and longer and dropped all the way to the floor and began spinning faster from Horace's mouth, unspooling by the yard. It began circling his feet, then quickly wound its way up around his legs, binding them together.

"It's—it's making a cocoon around you!" Auggie shouted.

Horace wanted to yell to his friends to get it off him, but he couldn't. And by the time he finally got the idea to try to tear the thread away, it was too late. The thread had already wound its way around his arms and was circling his chest. What was happening to him? Was he becoming a mummy? Horace's eyes darted around the room for an answer, but before he could think what to do, the thread had wound all the way around his neck and had completely covered his head.

Finally, the spinning of the thread stopped, and Horace's mouth felt clear of crawly things, cocoons, and the cupcake sock on his tongue. Yes, his mouth was free. Now his only problem was that he was stuck in a dark cocoon.

As he opened his mouth to yell to his friends, he suddenly became very tired and fell asleep.

● ● ●

Auggie and Xax stared at the shiny, black cocoon that held their friend.

"Do you think he's okay in there?" Xax asked.

Auggie swatted his brother on the shoulder. "Of course he's not okay! Something grew out of his mouth and swallowed him up." He ran to Horace's desk and grabbed a pair of scissors. "We have to cut him out before it gets worse. Who knows what could be going on inside there?"

"*Boys! Horace! How are you doing?*" a voice called from downstairs.

Auggie and Xax looked at each other, then back to Horace. It was Dr. Splattly, Horace's dad.

"What should we do about Horace?" Xax asked his brother in a terrified whisper.

The twins heard Dr. Splattly's footsteps on the stairs.

Auggie looked down at the notebook and kicked it under the bed. "Uh, just—just leave this to me and—and do what I do."

Dr. Splattly walked in the room. Auggie stood next to the cocoon and began patting it gently with his hand. He motioned for Xax to do the same thing.

Dr. Splattly stared. "Uh, boys, is something wrong? Where's Horace?"

Auggie stopped patting the cocoon and walked up to Dr. Splattly. "He's inside our cocoon. It's a science project. We're supposed to make a cocoon and see how it feels to be a caterpillar. Xax and I already tried it. Now it's Horace's turn."

Dr. Splattly walked up to the cocoon and gave it a rap with a fist. "Well, it looks very sturdy." He leaned close to it. "Hey, Horace! Growing any wings while you're in there? Are you becoming a moth or a butterfly?"

Xax and Auggie stared at the cocoon, waiting for it to answer.

A drop of sweat ran down Auggie's forehead.

Goose bumps broke out across Xax's arms.

Dr. Splattly looked to the twins, concerned. "Why isn't Horace answering?" he asked.

Auggie stepped forward again. "We're supposed to be pretending we're caterpillars, and since caterpillars can't talk, Horace isn't supposed to either. If he does, we'll have to report it to our teacher, and Horace will get a lower grade."

Dr. Splattly smiled. "Well, then I guess it's a good thing he didn't answer me, huh?" He leaned in close to the cocoon again. "Good work, Horace. See you in about an hour."

Dr. Splattly planted a hand on each twin's head, ruffled their hair, and walked downstairs to his office.

Auggie swooped his bangs over the top of his head and wiped beads of sweat off his forehead.

Xax shook his bangs over his eyes and began counting the goose bumps on his arms. He hadn't reached higher than twenty-three before a sound interrupted him.

Crrrrrkkkkk. The cocoon was opening.

THE TOWER OF HOT DOGS

Horace had woken up and stretched his arms and legs, forgetting where he was. *Crrrrrkkkkk.* His arms split the cocoon apart, and the bright light of the room met his eyes. Horace kept blinking, letting his eyes adjust to the light. He pushed the cocoon away from his body, and it fell to the floor.

Auggie and Xax shook him gently.

"Hey, Horace, are you all right?" Auggie asked.

"Do you think he's dead?" Xax asked his brother.

"If he was dead, how could he be moving and blinking?" Auggie asked, peering into Horace's eyes.

"Maybe he's almost dead," Xax argued. "Or maybe he's the walking dead, like a mummy!"

Horace's eyesight came into focus, and he could clearly see the twins and the worried expressions on their faces. "No, of course I'm not dead," he told them. "Or even almost dead." He pulled away from his friends and looked at the cocoon on his bedroom floor. "Boy, those cupcakes can make strange things happen. It was scary in there. I fell completely asleep."

"You were sleeping the whole time?" Auggie asked. "Even when your dad came in?"

Horace jumped with a start. "My dad saw the cocoon?"

Xax nodded. "But we thought really fast and told him it was a science experiment."

Auggie pointed to his head. "*I* thought really fast. Xax was as scared as a box of crackers at a parrot convention."

"I was just *pretending* to be scared as a diversionary tactic," Xax said, sitting on the bed.

Auggie ignored his brother. "So what are

your powers?" he asked Horace. "Do you feel anything?"

Horace began changing into his superhero costume. The hands of the costume were a bit torn from the shovel fingertips he had grown that afternoon. "Hold on a minute," he told his friends.

"Hold on to what?" Xax asked. "What's going to happen?"

Horace ran to Melody's room and found a pair of her purple mittens in her dresser drawer. He pulled them over his hands to cover up the holes, then rushed back to join his friends. "All fixed. Sort of."

"I never saw a superhero with mittens before," Xax said.

"Do you know what your powers are?" Auggie asked again.

Horace waved his arms around and kicked out his feet, waiting for something to happen. "Not yet," he said, pointing a finger into the air to see if he could fly. "Sometimes they come fast and sometimes slow. I'm sure I'll figure it out soon." He stood before the mirror and looked at himself. He didn't feel like he had any super-powers at all. "Do you think Melody could have just made that cupcake to trick me, and it only makes a cocoon?" he asked.

"I don't know," Xax said.

"Could be," Auggie said. "Your sister's pretty tricky."

Horace raised his arms, unfurling the wings of his costume and making a rustling noise. He waved his fingers. "The first time, when I ate the cupcakes, I just pointed my fingers and rose into the air." He turned to his friends and shrugged. "Maybe we should just walk down to the Hot Dog Hut and see what happened," he said.

He was reaching to peel the hood from his head when a flash of color in the mirror caught his attention. The skin around his eyes had turned black while half his face turned bright orange and the other half turned gray. "Oh, whoa! What's going on?" he asked. As he took a step toward the mirror, lightning bolts burst from his elbows and knees, blasting him off the floor. The lightning bolts shot around the room, bouncing off the walls, ceiling, and floor.

"Hey! What are you doing? What's happened to you?!" Auggie yelled as he ducked, bent, and twisted to get away from the lightning bolts.

"Yikes!" Xax cried after a bolt hit him in the butt.

"Yowee-zowee-zooks! Sorry," Horace said. "I didn't know. I guess I should only use this outside where they can't bounce off the walls and stuff." He went over to Xax. "Are you okay?"

Xax rubbed his behind. "I guess I'm okay, but it was like I'd been poked with a hot needle."

"You better be careful with that power," Auggie said. "I almost got hit in the eye. And your face looks really strange."

Horace folded his arms behind his back, making sure he didn't bend his elbows or knees. "Yeah, I know," he said. He looked in the mirror. "I think I kind of look like a cross between a monarch butterfly and some kind of moth," he said. He took off the mitten on his right hand. His skin was mostly orange, but there were three small black spots in the center of his palm. He took off the other mitten and saw that the skin of his left hand was gray but with three yellow spots in the center of his palm.

"Pretty creepy if you ask me," Auggie said.

"Do moths and butterflies really shoot lightning bolts?" Xax asked.

Horace shook his head. "Not any that I know of, but who knows what kind of things my sister might have put into the cupcake to make this happen to me. She's made some pretty scary ingredients with her Lily Deaver Spill & Brew Science Laboratory." He went to his bedroom window and looked out. The tower of hot dogs was still there. "Stand back," he warned the twins. "It's time to see if Prickles caused that hot-dog explosion."

Auggie and Xax stepped out of the room. Each boy carefully leaned in the doorframe to see what their superhero friend would do next.

Horace stuck his head out the window and extended his wings so his arms were perfectly straight. He then bent his arms and legs so his elbows and knees pointed at the floor. Instantly, four giant thunderbolts blasted from his body, rocketing the Cupcaked Crusader out of the house and into the sky.

• • •

Horace jetted through the air, lifting his wings and tilting his body to steer himself toward downtown Blootinville. He soared over Blootinville Elementary, where kids played on the Blootinball field, and past the Chef Nibbles factory, where Melody and her troop were at her Lily Deaver Scout meeting. Last time he flew, he had the power to fly like a plane and could control how he took off and landed. But now he wasn't like a plane. Now he was like a human cannonball shooting through the air. How would he stop himself from crashing into a building? He hadn't thought of that when he took off.

Horace soared closer and closer to the tower of hot dogs. It was cemented together with a mixture of ketchup, relish, and mustard. It was only ten yards from Horace, and he was closing in on it fast. In seconds, he would slam right into the frankfurters unless he figured a way to stop.

And he did.

Quickly, Horace bent his elbows and sent two colossal lightning bolts at the humongous tower. Instantly, the hot dogs sizzled and exploded, blasting the tower to smithereens. The Cupcaked Crusader had created a hailstorm of frankfurters! The hot dogs rained down on Horace, slowing his flight so he was able to bat his wings and drift to the ground. If not for the hot-dog meat, ketchup, mustard, and relish he was now wearing, it would have been a perfect landing.

Horace surveyed the scene. People were catching the hot dogs he had grilled with the lightning bolts and eating them happily. Prickles the porcupine, though, wasn't anywhere in sight.

"Thanks, Cupcaked Crusader," a woman said as she stuffed her mouth with a hot dog. "I needed a snack."

Dogs dashed around, eating the franks that fell to the ground. A group of boys tilted their heads back and caught the raining hot dogs in their open mouths.

Horace rushed over to Mr. Giles Tweetotter, the owner of the hot-dog stand. The shack was nowhere in sight. It was as if it had never existed. "What happened?" Horace asked. "Did a fire-breathing porcupine do this?"

"No-no-no," Mr. Tweetotter moaned. "It was a group of kids. Terrible, terrible hooligans," he cried. "I was serving hot dogs when all of a sudden they stormed the shack and began tearing the place apart with crowbars. I think they were just little kids. They were almost as small as you."

Horace frowned. "Well, I'm not *that* small, sir, so they must have been pretty big and strong," he said.

"Oh no, they *were* small," Mr. Tweetotter answered. "They overturned tables, then turned the temperature in my hot-dog boiler up so high that it exploded the whole restaurant and sent a giant cloud of steam in the air. Then they took all my hot dogs, mustard, ketchup, and relish and built that giant tower. They said it was a sign to everyone in Blootinville to stay away from here and not eat hot dogs ever again."

Horace helped Mr. Tweetotter sit on one of the remaining picnic benches. He was careful not to bend his arms or legs and shoot lightning bolts. "Where did the criminals go?" he asked. "Did they leave any clues behind?"

Mr. Tweetotter looked at the blackened pit where his hot-dog shack had stood. "They wore masks and ran around so quickly I never got a good look at them," he said sadly. "Now I'll have to build a new restaurant. I just hope those kids won't come back and destroy it."

Horace gave Mr. Tweetotter a pat on the shoulder. "I'll catch them before that happens, sir. Don't you worry."

"I hope you can, Cupcaked Crusader. I sure hope you can," he said.

Horace walked across the area, looking for a clue. Why would a bunch of miniature punks attack the hot-dog shack?

He stared at the ground and spotted a piece of torn purple cloth twisted around a hot dog. Was this a clue? He bent over, unwound the fabric from the meat, and slipped it in his wing pocket.

A bunch of cars screeched to a stop. TV news crews, newspaper reporters, and a group of police officers ran to Mr. Tweetotter. The hot-dog restaurant owner pointed to Horace. "The Cupcaked Crusader said he'd catch the people who did this," he said. The police and newspeople looked at Horace and began snapping pictures, shooting video, and asking questions.

"How will you do it?"

"Who do you think did it, Cupcaked Crusader?"

Horace didn't know the answer to any of the questions. What he did know was that he had better take off into the sky before the effects of the cupcake wore off and he had to walk home. He aimed his elbows and knees at the ground, blasted out four lightning bolts, and jetted into the sky.

Chapter 7

HORACE FLATTLY

Horace flapped his wings and steered in the direction of his house. Down below, tiny cars drove up and down the streets and people the size of ants walked the sidewalks and played in their yards. As he flew closer and closer to home, Horace began feeling lighter and lighter and thinner and thinner. When he looked at his body, he saw that the costume was now completely loose. He had suddenly grown as flat as a leaf! He couldn't lift an arm or leg. He was so thin, he could feel the air blowing right through his body. Horace hoped it wouldn't get too windy, or he might just float all the way out of Blootinville.

Then Horace thought about his head. Had it become as flat as a balloon after it's been popped?

Horace crossed his eyes and checked his nose, then stuck out his tongue. Yep, both still looked the same as usual. He thought of the hardest math problem he could: $2{,}349 \times 9{,}035{,}472 \div 654 = \textit{What?}$ Horace thought hard but couldn't come up with an answer. But since he *could* think, and since he *could* still see his nose and tongue, he was pretty sure his head and brain hadn't flattened like the rest of him.

The loose costume flapped around his butterfly-thin body. Horace pointed his elbows, but only tiny sparks blew out. All he could do was float through the sky like a falling leaf. Was this what his sister warned him about when she said eating too much of a cupcake could make the powers mutate?

He stared down at his house, sinking lower and lower until he landed gently on the roof of the garage. He lay there, flat and unable to move. His body felt so thin, he was sure that if someone wanted, they could fold him up and slip him in an envelope. Is this why Melody said he shouldn't try cupcakes without her around to supervise? Maybe the cupcakes could be more dangerous than he'd thought.

Horace lifted his head. "Auggie! Xax!" he called in a small voice. "Auggie! Xax!" It was hard to yell loudly when his lungs were as small as empty balloons.

Horace didn't hear a response.

A wind blew and lifted Horace off the garage roof and toward the back of the house. He floated by his bedroom window and saw the twins sitting on the bed. "Hey, guys!" he yelled as loud as he could. "Come get me. I'm floating down in the backyard."

The two boys turned their heads.

"Is that Horace?" Auggie asked.

"It looks like a purple rag, but it sure sounds like Horace," Xax said.

"It *is* me," Horace yelled as he sank to the ground. "Come carry me inside."

• • •

Auggie and Xax changed their friend out of his Cupcaked Crusader costume and into a T-shirt and jeans.

"You're so thin, this is kind of like playing with paper dolls," Xax said.

"Be careful and don't tear me," Horace replied. "I'm not sure real people can be fixed with tape."

Auggie tickled Horace's ear. "Hey, if you sneeze or laugh too hard, you tear yourself to pieces?" he asked.

"I don't know and let's not try to find out, okay?" Horace replied.

The twins propped Horace's body up on the bed so it looked like he was sitting with his back against the headboard. They even placed the latest edition of the magazine *Your Gym Teacher's a Bloodsucking Toad* in his lap so he'd look like he was doing something. Horace peered into his long mirror. "I still don't look normal," he said. "My eyes and skin have changed back, but I'm still all flat, and my clothes are way too baggy. Maybe you should stuff my shirt and pants with pillows."

"I don't understand this superpower at all," Auggie said. "What good is being flat?"

Xax nodded, shaking his hair over his eyes. "The toilet paper at home isn't as thin as you."

Baroop—baroop! A car horn honked from outside. Auggie and Xax grabbed their backpacks off the floor.

"That's Claudius with the limo," Xax said. "It's time for us to go home."

Auggie looked at Horace. "Will you be all right? Will the power wear off soon?"

Horace sighed. "Probably. But we haven't even had time to discuss everything I found out."

Baroop—baroop!

Xax raced out the door and downstairs.

"Sorry, Horace, but we gotta go," Auggie apologized to his flat friend. "Let's have a conference call later." He slipped his backpack over his shoulders and dashed out of the room.

Horace lay back on the bed and stared at himself in the mirror. What else could a flat superhero with no muscles do?

• • •

Fortunately the powers of the caterpillar cupcake wore off a few minutes after the Blootins left. By the time Horace's father checked on him between patients, Horace was back to being his normal, little full-bodied self.

He crushed up the cocoon and hid it in the

trash, then spent the rest of the afternoon doing schoolwork. At 5:30, he heard Melody come home from her Lily Deaver meeting. Instead of barging into her brother's room and picking on him like she usually did, Melody went straight into her own room. Horace knocked on her door.

"Are you okay in there?" he asked.

"Of course I'm okay," Melody called through the door. "Now leave me alone. I'm quite busy."

"Aren't you going to start cooking dinner?" he asked. "Dad's with his last patient, and Mom will be home at seven."

"Don't you worry about it. Just go down and set the table," she ordered.

"What about the cupcakes? It would be great to have some with superpowers that did neat stuff and didn't make you flat," he hinted, hoping he wasn't being too obvious. "Do you think you'll be making any new ones soon?" he asked.

"I'm not making any more ever," Melody called. "And stop bothering me."

"Grump," Horace muttered at her. He went

downstairs and watched TV. On the news, there was an interview with Mr. Tweetotter, who was very upset about his store being destroyed. "But the Cupcaked Crusader appeared and said he'd find who did this and make sure it never happens again," he told the reporter.

Thinkthinkthink, Horace told himself. What could he do? The people of Blootinville were expecting the Cupcaked Crusader to come to the rescue. But how could he do it if his sister wouldn't make any more cupcakes?

Chapter 8

CHEF NIBBLES' CANNED SNOODLES AND CHEAZE

Dr. Hinkle Splattly, Mari Splattly, and Horace sat at the dining-room table, waiting for Melody to serve dinner.

"Well, at the paper everyone was upset about what happened to the Hot Dog Hut," Mrs. Splattly said. It was a rule that every night at dinner, the Splattlys would each talk about what happened that day. Horace's dad called it "Sharing Time." He said it was important to express your thoughts and feelings so you got them out of your head. "Sometimes an empty head is a good head," he was fond of saying.

"A reporter at the paper said the Cupcaked Crusader appeared on the scene," Horace's mom said. "Thank goodness he's here to help."

"Why would anyone want to destroy the Hot Dog Hut?" Dr. Splattly asked. "Doesn't everyone like hot dogs?"

Melody entered the room carrying a steaming bowl of food. "I made Chef Nibbles' Canned Snoodles and Cheaze," she said with a smile. "It comes right out of a big can—you don't even have to add water." She spooned a big glop of

Snoodles on the center of everyone's plate. The Snoodles were like noodles, only gray and slimy. The Cheaze sauce looked like cheese sauce but had chunks of green furry stuff in it.

Melody served herself, then sat at her seat, placing the serving bowl in the center of the table. "Inhale that scintillating aroma," she said cheerfully. "You can't get fine food like this using natural ingredients. A smell like this can only be made with chemicals."

"Honey, is something wrong?" Mrs. Splattly asked. "You've never made dinner from a can before. You won't even drink soda from a can."

Dr. Splattly poked the Snoodles with a fork. "Melody, didn't you say that the Lily Deaver handbook says you can never cook dinner from a can? I thought all Lily Deaver Scouts had to make everything from scratch."

Melody dug her fork into the pile of Snoodles on her plate and shoved them into her mouth. Cheaze sauce dripped down over her chin along with a glob of green furry stuff. "I don't care what the Lily Deaver rules are. Now that I've met Chef Nibbles, I'm beginning to think cooking fancy foods isn't so much fun anymore. I'm thinking that from now on we'll have Chef Nibbles' Canned Snoodles and Cheaze every night of the week."

Horace's jaw dropped. "Every night? Are you crazy?" he asked.

"Once a year will be plenty of Snoodles and Cheaze," Mrs. Splattly said to her daughter.

"Are you tired of making dinner? Would you like us to share cooking duties?" Dr. Splattly asked.

Melody slammed her fork to the table. "I do want to do the cooking. And I want all the cooking to be Chef Nibbles' Snoodles and Cheaze."

Dr. Splattly took a bite of his Snoodles and frowned. "Actually, Melody, that is not okay. I think we like to have different things for dinner. You used to enjoy making up recipes and using your Lily Deaver oven. Why has that changed?"

Melody ate more of her dinner. "I've just

decided that it's time we ate Chef Nibbles' Canned Snoodles and Cheaze. I'm tired of all my Lily Deaver junk. I think I'm going to resign from the Lily Deaver troop anyway. All the second-grade girls are. We want to become Junior Nibblettes."

"What's a Nibblette?" Mrs. Splattly asked.

Melody smiled and sat up in her chair. "Followers of Chef Nibbles. He's starting his own troop of Junior Nibblettes. The uniforms are tomato-sauce orange. Last week he gave all the Lily Deaver girls in our troop Chef Nibbles cell phones." Melody finished her dinner, then stood and held up a foot. "Today he gave us Chef Nibbles tomato-sauce orange cowboy boots. Aren't they superlicious?" She smiled and did a kick in the air. "I'm going up to my room to pack up all that silly Lily Deaver stuff." She skipped out of the dining room and upstairs to her bedroom.

Horace looked to his mother and father. "I thought all that Lily Deaver stuff was crazy," he said, then he picked up a forkful of Snoodles and Cheaze. "But I have a feeling this Chef Nibbles guy is far worse."

• • •

That evening, Horace sat at his desk with his schoolbooks but couldn't concentrate. Why was Melody so excited about Snoodles and Cheaze? And Mr. Tweetotter said the people who destroyed the Hot Dog Hut didn't want people to eat hot dogs anymore? It was all too weird.

He got up from his desk and went to his closet, where he hid the superhero outfit. He unzipped the pocket and took out the strip of purple fabric he found at the Hot Dog Hut. He had seen this color somewhere before, but couldn't remember exactly where.

Thinkthinkthink, he told himself. He rubbed the fabric back and forth between his fingers. Purplepurplepurple, thinkthinkthink.

And then it hit him . . . the fabric wasn't purple. It was *lavender*, which was a particular shade of purple!

Who wore lavender and had said she was

visiting the Chef Nibbles' Canned Food factory today? Who wanted everyone to eat Chef Nibbles' Canned Snoodles and Cheaze for dinner every night?

Lily Deaver Scout number zero-one-two-zero-six-three:

Melody Splattly.

• • •

Horace tucked the scrap of the Lily Deaver lavender uniform in his pocket and walked to his sister's room, knocking on the door. "Hey, I'm coming in," he called, not waiting for an answer in case she told him not to. Horace opened the door and found his sister standing in the middle of the floor, trying to stuff her lavender Lily Deaver Stitch & Thread Sewing Machine into a box already packed with her lavender Lily Deaver Spill & Brew Science Laboratory, her lavender Lily Deaver laptop computer, and her lavender Lily Deaver Cook & Bake Oven with all her special cupcake ingredients. Crumpled on the floor in a ball was one of the seven Lily Deaver uniforms she usually washed and ironed every day and would never let touch the ground.

"I didn't tell you to come in," Melody said.

Horace walked over and peered down into the box, then looked around the room. Melody's room and furniture were painted lavender, with a row of white and pink tulips stenciled along the walls. She used to love Lily Deaver so much, she'd cried until her parents bought her the Lily Deaver Canopy Bed, where she slept every night. Now the only thing on Melody's lavender Lily Deaver desk was her new bright orange Chef Nibbles cell phone. And on her lavender carpet in the corner was a large can of wall and ceiling paint. CHEF NIBBLES' CANNED AND COLD ROTTEN TOMATO SNOODLE SOUP & WALL PAINT, the label read.

Did this mean Melody wouldn't be making any more cupcakes?

Did this mean Horace's days as a superhero were over?

Horace picked up Melody's uniform off the

floor. "So now you don't like Lily Deaver? Yowee-zowee-zooks! What's up with *that*?" he asked.

Melody sneered. "Lily Deaver's for babies. Chef Nibbles is much more sophisticated."

Horace examined the uniform in his hand. One sleeve was torn, and the skirt was smeared with mustard and ketchup stains. He thought about the explosion at the Hot Dog Hut and Mr. Tweetotter saying that the people who had destroyed it were little, but not as little as Horace. "Were you at the Hot Dog Hut this afternoon when it exploded?" he asked.

"Of course not," Melody said. "I was with Chef Nibbles and the other Lily Deaver girls at his factory."

"Then how did your uniform get torn and dirty with mustard and ketchup stains?" Horace asked. He pulled the strip of torn fabric from his pocket and held it up to the torn sleeve of Melody's Lily Deaver uniform. "And how come the tear on your dress matches this piece of fabric I found at the scene of the crime?"

Melody grabbed the uniform from her brother and tossed it onto her bed. "You're crazy. Don't you think I would have remembered if I'd been there? My uniform got dirty when we were cooking at the factory. Now please excuse yourself from my room."

Horace gazed at his sister. She didn't look like she was lying. She looked like she really believed she'd been at the factory all afternoon. Could it be true? But then why would Horace have found the torn piece of her dress at the Hot Dog Hut?

Blip-blip. Blippety-blip-blip.

Melody's cell phone rang, and she ran to it, flipping it open.

Horace watched her. Just like this afternoon when Melody answered the phone, a very serious expression crossed her face and she spoke in a strange, robotlike voice. "Lily Deaver Scout number zero-one-two-zero-six-three reporting. Yes, sir. The factory at midnight. Yes, sir." She pushed a button, then closed the phone.

Horace backed out of the room and shut the door.

The factory at midnight?

He had a feeling the Cupcaked Crusader would be there, too. He went downstairs to call Auggie and Xax immediately. This was too big a job for a superhero to tackle alone.

THE CAN MAN'S PLAN

The Cupcaked Crusader flipped down his kick-stand and parked his bike by the Chef Nibbles' Canned Food factory. A thought crossed his mind: Did other superheroes ever have to travel by bicycle? Horace wasn't sure. But then Horace didn't think most superheroes ate cupcakes baked by their sisters to get superpowers. And since he was now a superhero with no cupcakes, he had to rely on pedal power to get him where he needed to go.

Horace checked his watch. The time was 11:58 P.M. Xax and Auggie should be meeting him here in two minutes, just in time for them to see what his sister was up to.

He looked up to see the factory glimmering in the moonlight. The building looked like a giant can with no label. It stood over one hundred feet high and was as long as a football field. On top of the building, a bright orange sign stood. CHEF NIBBLES CANNED FOOD FACTORY, it read in giant letters. And underneath those words, in smaller letters: *Soon-to-Be the World Famous Chef Nibbles Canned Food Factory*.

"What's going on?"

"Hey, trip."

Horace jumped at the sound of Xax and Auggie's voices. He turned to see the twins lean their two-person bicycle against a tree. They were wearing their costumes from Halloween last year. Auggie was dressed like a frog. He wore a green rubber shirt, pants, and mask. Xax was dressed like George Washington and wore a powdered white wig, a long blue tailcoat, and a frilly white blouse.

"Why are you dressed like that?" Horace asked.

"We're in disguise," Xax said.

"You get to wear a costume, so why can't we?" Auggie asked.

"But I'm a superhero," Horace explained. "I have to be in disguise."

"Well, we're superhero helpers," Auggie said. "I'm Frogman, able to leap high in the air." He hopped in the air and laughed.

Xax smiled. "And I'm Super-President-Man. I can recite all three thousand, one hundred words of the twenty-seven amendments of the Constitution in two hours, forty-four minutes, and thirty-nine seconds."

"That's not a superpower," his brother told him.

"I think it is," Xax answered. "And it's better than being some dumb frog who can only jump a few inches in the air."

Auggie leaped as high as he could. "See, that was nearly ten feet."

"More like ten inches," Xax replied.

Auggie stepped toward his brother. "Yeah, well, how much of a help are you going to be if a bad guy comes? You'll just stand there and

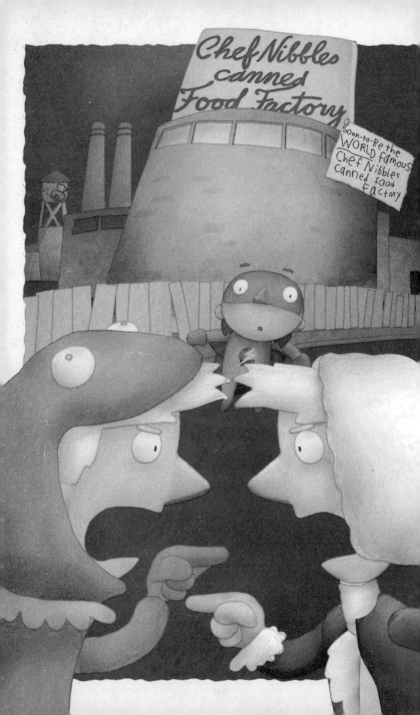

tell him the Declaration of Independence."

Xax stepped angrily toward his brother. "I know the amendments to the Constitution, not the Declaration of Independence," Xax corrected.

Auggie looked to Horace. "If a bad guy comes, Xax is going to bore him to death," he teased.

Xax frowned and took a step closer to his brother. Horace stepped between the twins before a fight broke out. "Come on, guys," he said. "We have to head inside and see what's going on. We're a team, remember?"

Xax and Auggie gave each other a cold stare, then followed Horace toward the factory.

• • •

The boys crept around the factory until they found the front door where the workers entered.

"It's locked," Horace said.

"Now what'll we do?" Xax asked.

"Don't you have any powers to bust it open?" Auggie asked Horace.

"Remember? I'm out of cupcakes. That's why I had to ride my bike here," Horace answered.

"Without those cupcakes, you're just an ordinary kid like us," Xax said.

Horace sighed. "I know—I know."

The three boys walked around the side of the building and saw the loading dock, a giant opening twenty feet high and thirty feet wide. Empty trucks pulled up to the loading dock every day and were filled with Chef Nibbles' Canned Foods. The trucks delivered the cans to stores all over Blootinville. Now the space was completely empty. Horace, Xax, and Auggie sneaked up the steps to the loading platform. At the far end was an open door with light spilling out onto the floor.

They approached the door, peeked around the frame, and gasped at what they saw.

In the center of a giant room sat a huge pot with tubes and pipes sticking out of it. The pipes were attached to fifty smaller pots that had tubes and pipes sticking out of them that attached to hundreds of even smaller pots. The smaller pots had tubes and pipes sticking out of them that were attached to small cans with labels for Chef Nibbles' Snoodles and Cheaze. Thousands of cans were waiting to be filled. At one end of the room, thousands of cartons marked CHEF NIBBLES' SNOODLES AND CHEAZE sat waiting to be delivered to stores.

Standing around all these pots and pipes and cans were twenty second-grade girls. All of them were dressed in black, just like Melody. All of the girls held bright orange Chef Nibbles cell phones in their hands. Before the girls stood a man who couldn't have been taller than Horace. He wore a white apron and chef's hat and stood on a stage so he could look down at the girls standing on the floor. Just like the man on the Chef Nibbles can, this man had a round face. And just like on the can, he had a long Snoodle strand dangling out of his mouth and hanging over his chin. Tomato sauce was splattered all over his cheeks.

"My dear, dear Nibblettes, thank you for coming to my lovely factory." Chef Sven Nibbles welcomed the girls in a loud voice. Every time he spoke, the strand of spaghetti hanging out of his mouth flipped around and slapped him on the cheek, chin, or forehead. He began speaking again, and the spaghetti strand whipped up and hit him in the nose. "At one P.M. tomorrow, I will call you on your cell phones and give you the order to attack. You will then start your mission to destroy all the supermarkets, restaurants, candy stores, ice-cream shops, and other places where people get food in this town."

He smiled. "And make sure you wear your Lily Deaver outfits and tell everyone that Lily Deaver ordered you to destroy the food shops." Nibbles held up a lavender tote bag, reached inside, and took out a small snack cup like the kind packed in school lunches. "Each of these fake Lily Deaver bags holds fifty of my little snack cups. Once you pop the lid, immediately throw the cup into the stores. It will explode a

gooey, sticky gravy that will cover everyone and everything within twenty feet. By the end of the afternoon, there will be nowhere left to get food. Everyone will be running to buy my Snoodles and Cheaze, and Lily Deaver will be blamed for the entire disaster!"

The twenty second-grade girls jumped and cheered. "No more Lily Deaver!" they shouted. "Down with Lily Deaver! Up with Chef Nibbles! Hooray for the Nibblettes!"

Chef Nibbles waved a hand, silencing the girls. "On your way back to your homes tonight, I want you to stop by your school and toss some cans into the cafeteria. Then for lunch tomorrow, all the kids will have to eat Chef Nibbles' Canned Snoodles and Cheaze!"

The girls clapped their hands. "Chef Nibbles! Chef Nibbles! Chef Nibbles!" they shouted.

"Girls, let's gravy-nate all of Blootinville! Let the gravy flow!" Nibbles cheered, pumping his little fist in the air.

Horace, Auggie, and Xax watched the girls

get more and more excited as Chef Nibbles began handing them their bags filled with the dangerous gravy snack packs.

"If his plan works, we'll have to eat Snoodles and Cheaze for the rest of our lives," Horace told his friends.

Auggie shook his head. "I'd rather starve. I hate Snoodles and Cheaze."

Xax nodded. "Twenty bags with fifty cans? That's one thousand gravy explosions. And if each one covers twenty square feet, that equals twenty thousand square feet of gooey, gravy ground."

"How are we going to stop them?" Auggie asked.

Horace shook his head and saw that the girls were heading for the door where they stood. "I'm not exactly sure, but we better come up with a plan before one o'clock tomorrow or this town's going to be one big, sticky gravy mess."

Chapter 10

THE ALL-NIGHT BAKE-A-THON

Xax and Auggie rode their bike home. Horace hopped on his and raced to the Splattly house as fast as he could. He wanted to ride by the school and see what the girls were up to, but he also knew he had other business to attend to before his sister got home. He needed more cupcakes.

Melody wasn't baking them anymore, which meant that tonight Horace would have to figure out how to make those special desserts so he'd have the powers to defeat Chef Nibbles and his Nibblettes.

Horace parked his bike in the garage and rushed into the basement. In the corner of the room was the Lily Deaver equipment his sister had put away earlier that evening. He picked up the box, carried it to his room, and glanced at his clock radio with the built-in tissue holder, toothpaste dispenser, and bird feeder. The time was 1:29 A.M. Six hours before he had to get up for school tomorrow and eleven hours and thirty-one minutes before the Nibblettes would begin their attack.

Horace plugged his sister's Lily Deaver Cook & Bake Oven into the wall and took out the special baking ingredients she used to mix her cupcake batter.

There were jars filled with all sorts of strange, colorful powders. There were small containers containing dried bugs, rubber bands, eyelashes, sparkling rocks, and about fifty more ingredients that only Melody knew how to use. The only thing missing in the box was a recipe book, but Horace knew his sister didn't use recipes. She made them up herself and remembered them in her head so no one could steal them.

Horace eyed the ingredients curiously. What to do? Where to begin? He'd never really baked anything before except for when he was five years old and he and his dad had made a horse-radish-celernip pie for the Celernip Festival.

But that was just a pie. He'd never baked cupcakes that gave people superpowers. Only his sister could do that.

But now he would try.

He blinked his tired eyes and gave his head a smack with an open palm to keep himself awake. It was going to be one long, confusing, yawn-filled night of cupcake experimentation, he thought.

Horace wondered if other superheroes ever had to borrow their sisters' kiddie ovens to bake cupcakes and save the world.

Probably not.

• • •

Horace spent the next four hours mixing, blend-ing, icing, and decorating. One batch of the cupcakes came out of the oven so burned that the minute Horace touched them with a finger, they crumbled to ashes. Another batch exploded the second he put them in the oven. Finally, on his third try, he was able to make two cupcakes. They were probably the worst cupcakes Horace had ever seen, but they were the best he could do. He'd just have to eat them and hope they worked as well as his sister's did. And maybe they wouldn't get him stuck in a cocoon or make him sing a teapot song.

The first cupcake was puffy and rippled. It looked like a stack of quarter-size pancakes covered with red icing. Hundreds of little blue wings stuck out from all over its top and sides. Horace was hoping this cupcake would help him fly.

The second cupcake was a bright, bright orange. It was shaped like a box and its sides were dented, like a car that's been dropped off a cliff. Growing out of the top of the cake were four tiny black trees with even tinier leaves.

Horace was hoping this one would make him grow as big and tall as a tree.

By 5:30 in the morning, Horace had cleaned up the mess and returned all the equipment and ingredients to the basement. He got exactly one hour and thirty-three minutes of sleep before his father called him down for breakfast.

Horace pumped a squirt of his favorite Celernip-Sparkle-Brite tooth gel and hair paste from his clock radio onto his toothbrush and brushed his teeth. A couple minutes later, he took a second squirt and rubbed it across the top of his head, making his short spiky hair stick straight up in the air. He slipped the cupcakes he made in the side pocket of his knapsack, then stuffed his costume in the main compartment under his books.

At the kitchen table, both Horace and Melody yawned as they ate their bowls of Celernos cereal and drank their glasses of Splinter celernip juice. Melody wore a clean Lily Deaver uniform.

"Why are you kids so tired?" Dr. Splattly asked. "Didn't you get enough sleep?"

Melody covered her mouth as she yawned again. "I got a perfect night's sleep."

Horace sat up in his chair and gazed at his sister, searching for some clue that she had been at the school and gravy-nated the cafeteria.

Melody tossed a crust of toast at her brother. "Please remove your eyes from my face."

"Stop staring at your sister," Dr. Splattly ordered.

Horace leaned over and examined Melody's

hair. He thought he spied specks of gravy stuck on the ends. "What's that stuff?" he asked, pulling on a strand.

Melody slapped his hand away. "Don't mess with my hairdo!" she squealed. She twisted the ends of her hair and tried to pull the brown stuff off. "It must be dust or something."

Horace wondered what the cafeteria must look like. Would Principal Nosair have to cancel school until they cleaned it up? Horace knew he didn't want to eat Snoodles and Cheaze or have every restaurant in town ruined by the gravy, but he did like the idea of a few days off from school. "Do you really not remember a thing about last night?" he asked.

Melody glared at her brother. "I remember that I slept in my bed." She turned to her father. "I think Horace gets stupider and stupider each day, don't you, Daddy?"

Horace gazed deep into her eyes. "I want to know where you went last night," he said, imitating Chef Nibbles' voice.

"What are you talking about, Horace? And

why are you talking like that?" Mrs. Splattly asked. "You know Melody was asleep in her bed just like you."

"Stop picking on your sister and eat your breakfast," Dr. Splattly said.

Melody picked up her plate and brought it to the sink. "Everyone, remember that I have another troop meeting. Today we're officially becoming Nibblettes and getting our new orange uniforms."

Mrs. Splattly went over to the refrigerator to read the school lunch menu. "Chef Nibbles is certainly devoting a lot of time to you girls."

"He's absolutely fascinating," Melody said. "Did you know that every can of Snoodles and Cheaze contains over one thousand chemicals, twenty-nine preservatives, and six kinds of plastic?"

"Plastic?" Horace asked.

Melody rolled her eyes. "Of course, ninny. How do you think the Snoodles get that exquisite slippery texture? They're sprayed with a special plastic coating."

"Lunch today is pizza, kiddos. I guess that

means you'll both be buying, right?" Mrs. Splattly opened her pocketbook.

Horace thought about the school cafeteria. "Uh, I might want to bring my lunch today."

"You love pizza," Dr. Splattly said. He looked at his watch. "And you don't have time to make lunch anyway. Just take your money and head off to school."

Horace frowned. "I have a feeling lunch won't be pizza today," he told his father.

"Why's that?" Mrs. Splattly asked.

Horace glanced at Melody. "Let's just say I have a feeling the menu's been changed."

Chapter 11

HAVE YOU EVER SEEN
A SCHOOL COOK CRY?

Principal Nosair and the school cook stood in the school yard with all the students and teachers. Everyone peered through the cafeteria windows with shocked expressions on their faces. The cafeteria door was blocked with chairs so no one could enter and step up to their knees in goopy gravy.

"It's the worst thing I've ever seen!" Chef Quaquaqua moaned. Tears rolled down his face as he sobbed into his hands. "The stove, the trays, the pots and pans, the tables and benches are covered with thick, gloppy gobs of gravy." He pointed into the room. "The walls and ceiling are dripping with gravy. And no matter how much I scrub, it won't come off!" He wiped tears from his eyes, then ran to the nurse's office to lie down.

"Does this mean you'll have to cancel school?" Horace asked.

"Cancel school? Oh no. Not ever," Principal Nosair told him. "Everyone will just have to eat lunch in the gymnasium until the cafeteria is repaired."

"What will we have to eat if there's no pizza?" Sara Willow asked. Today, her hair hung down past her shoulders and was streaked with silver paint and decorated with baby-pink roses.

Cyrus Splinter poked a finger at Horace's head. Cyrus was the big bully of Blootinville Elementary. He was the tallest kid in the school by half a foot and the meanest by eleven and a half yards. "If Horace Splattly doesn't eat lunch, he may shrink to be even smaller than a two-year-old."

"I'm not shrinking," Horace called. "I grew one whole inch last week."

"No, you didn't," Melody announced. "My puny ten-year-old brother is exactly the same size he's been since he was four years old."

"That's not true!" Horace shouted. "I've grown three inches since I was five!"

The entire school laughed. Even Sara Willow was chuckling with her friends.

Principal Nosair gave Horace a pat on the head. "Don't worry, Horace. We'll make sure you have lunch. Fortunately for us, Chef Nibbles was driving by the school early this morning with a van full of Canned Snoodles and Cheaze. He delivered us enough to last for months."

The second-grade Lily Deaver Scouts cheered.

The rest of the school moaned.

Horace looked at Auggie and Xax. "I think we better come up with a plan before Snoodles and Cheaze is all there is left to eat for the rest of our lives."

• • •

As the school day passed, things didn't get any better for Horace.

In history, Ms. Goldentoe spoke. "Mr.

Splattly, during the Revolutionary War, who said, 'Give me liberty or give me death'?"

Horace was so busy working on a plan to stop the Lily Deaver girls from gravy-nating the town that he answered with the first thing that came into his head. "Chef Nibbles."

The class exploded with laughter.

"It's not that funny," Horace said.

"Please pay attention, Mr. Splattly," Ms. Goldentoe told him.

Horace slumped in his chair.

In science class, Mr. Dienow asked Horace where to put a plant so it would grow fastest.

Horace had been so busy thinking about where he would change into his Cupcaked Crusader costume that he answered with the first thing that came into his head.

"In the bathroom toilet stall."

The class exploded with laughter.

"I think his brain's in the toilet," Cyrus Splinter said.

Mr. Dienow tossed a stick of chalk to the floor in anger. "Well, Horace Splattly, since *you're* so little, why don't we put you in the toilet for the last twenty minutes of class and see if you grow?"

"That's the funniest thing I ever heard," Sara Willow told a friend.

Horace turned red with embarrassment and glared at Mr. Dienow. If only he could let everyone know how evil their science teacher really was. *And* how he once tried to take over the world. But if Horace told them, everyone would know he was the Cupcaked Crusader. . . . Horace shook his head and kept his mouth shut. It was tough being a superhero when no one understood that he had more important things on his mind than science and history.

• • •

During lunch, the kids who hadn't brought food from home had to eat Chef Nibbles' Canned Snoodles and Cheaze. Horace, Auggie, and Xax sat at a table in the corner of the gym and stared into their bowls. The Snoodles looked even more gray than the Snoodles at dinner last night. The Cheaze sauce had even bigger chunks of green furry stuff in it.

The boys dipped their spoons into the bowls and took bites of the Snoodles.

Xax and Auggie gasped, then spat the food into their napkins.

"This tastes grosser than glue and wet newspaper," Auggie said.

"And it's the color of dead people," Xax said. "Do you think maybe it's dead people's brains?"

All the kids ate their Snoodles and Cheaze with sad, snarling faces.

That is, all the kids except for a table of second-grade girls in one corner of the room. The Lily Deaver troop sat wearing their lavender Lily Deaver outfits and eating the Snoodles and Cheaze clean to the bottoms of their bowls. The girls rubbed their tummies and smiled. "Ohhhhh, it's so goooooood!" they moaned happily. "I can't wait to eat this every, every day! More Snoodles and Cheaze, please!"

Horace looked to the clock on the wall.

Twelve o'clock. In one hour, the Lily Deaver girls would get the call from Chef Nibbles that would send them running around town, destroying all the food markets and restaurants.

Horace stood and grabbed his backpack from under the table. "Guys, I think we have to stop Nibbles right now."

Xax started shaking. "You saw what that gravy did to the cafeteria," he said. "What if Chef Nibbles tells the girls to throw gravy snack cups at *us*? Maybe we should wait until tomorrow and see if—"

Auggie and Horace yanked Xax to his feet and dragged him into the hall. "There's no time to wait," Auggie said.

"We have to get moving," Horace added. He walked to the boys' bathroom. "You guys stand guard and don't let anyone in. I'll change into my costume and eat the cupcakes. Then when I come out, I'll head over to the canned food factory to get Nibbles' phone before he can contact the Lily Deaver Scouts. While I'm there, you guys steal all the Lily Deaver troop's tote bags with the snack cups."

"Good plan," Auggie said.

"I think a better plan would be just to eat Snoodles and Cheaze," Xax suggested. "It really wasn't so bad, was it?"

Auggie ignored his brother and looked at his watch. "It's ten minutes after twelve, Horace. We better get a move on."

Horace pushed open the door to the bathroom, but just as he was about to step in, someone else stepped out.

"Hello, chaps," a short man said, stepping into the hall. The man was about as tall as Horace and was dressed in a white apron and chef's hat. He had a big, round face, and a long Snoodle strand dangled out of his mouth and hung over his chin. Tomato sauce was splattered all over his cheeks.

Horace, Auggie, and Xax stared with surprise.

"Why lookee lookee here—my favorite mayor's twin boys," the man said with a wide grin. He held out both his hands and grabbed hold of each of the twins' hands, giving them a shake. "I've seen your picture in your father's office. Don't you recognize my face? I'm Chef Nibbles. How do you do?" And as he spoke, the Snoodle strand whipped up and stuck to the tip of his nose.

INTO THE BATHROOM

Chef Nibbles clapped a hand on each twin's back. "I can't wait to tell your father I met his sons. I'll have to invite your family to the factory for a special tasting of Burboil Casserole. It's my newest food creation. It's only in the testing phase, but I'm hoping to have it canned and in stores in time for Thanksgiving. It's going to replace turkey on dinner tables everywhere."

Auggie looked at Xax.

Xax looked at Auggie.

"Uh, that sounds delicious, sir," Auggie said with a trembling voice.

"Are you really friends with our dad?" Xax asked with fear in his eyes.

Chef Nibbles laughed. "Of course I am! Your father cut the Snoodle ribbon at the opening of my factory last year. We've been friends ever since."

"He never told us," Auggie said.

The chef smiled. "Well, no matter. Did you enjoy your lunch of Snoodles and Cheaze?"

"Uh, yes, sir," Auggie said, trying to sound like he meant it.

"Yes, Mr. Nibbles, sir," Xax answered. "We couldn't get enough, we love it so much."

Chef Nibbles smiled as wide as an ocean, grabbed the twins by their hands, and led them back toward the gym. "Well, then let's get you each another bowlful. Your father would never forgive me if I let his growing boys go hungry."

Horace gasped as his friends were led away by the chef. The second they were out of sight, he dashed through the bathroom door and into a toilet stall. He unpacked his Cupcaked Crusader outfit from his backpack and changed from his school clothes.

And while he did this, he thought about his

plan. It would have to change now that Chef Nibbles had come to the school and was hanging out with Auggie and Xax.

Horace pulled the hood of the costume over his head and slipped on the two purple mittens to cover the holes in the hands.

Bwoop—bwoop—bwoop! The sound of the fire alarm filled the school. A bright red light flashed around the bathroom. *Bwoop—bwoop—bwoop!*

"All students and adults please evacuate the building," Principal Nosair called over the loudspeaker.

Horace stepped out of the toilet stall and took a sniff. He didn't smell smoke, but that didn't mean there wasn't a fire somewhere in the school. What should he do? He certainly couldn't leave the bathroom in his Cupcaked Crusader costume and go out to the school yard.

Not without superpowers.

He reached into his bag and took out the cupcakes he had made.

There was the puffy red one that looked like a stack of tiny pancakes with little wings and the bright orange one shaped like a busted-up box with four little trees growing out of it.

What would the cupcakes do? Horace hadn't a clue. But what he did know was that he needed all the powers he could get in order to stop Chef Nibbles from calling the Lily Deaver girls.

And Horace thought eating two whole cupcakes was the only way to do it. If the cupcakes made him flat as a pancake or hurt him, that was just a risk this superhero would have to take.

Horace took the orange cupcake with the four little trees, gave it a curious glance, then popped it in his mouth.

Horace smiled. The cupcake may have looked weird, but it tasted like warm orange pudding. Maybe he was as good as his sister at making the cupcakes and didn't need her to bake them anymore. After all, if she didn't want her special ingredients or Lily Deaver oven, he could keep them in his room.

Horace chewed and swallowed, then opened his mouth and looked into the mirror above the row of sinks. All that was left in his mouth were the four tiny black trees. They stood on his tongue with their branches poking the roof of his mouth. The trees began dropping their leaves. They fell to Horace's tongue and dissolved, tasting exactly like licorice. Then the oddest thing happened. Horace felt roots begin to grow from the trees in and around his tongue. He tried wiggling his tongue to get them off. But the harder he tried to poke them away, the faster their roots grew. They kept growing longer and thicker, slithering through and around his tongue, down his throat, and deep into his chest. He could feel the roots encircle his lungs like snakes, squeezing the air out of them.

Maybe he wasn't such a great baker after all, Horace thought.

He clutched his throat and gasped for air. He opened his mouth and tried to yank the tiny trees out, but they only thrashed their sharp branches at his hands, scratching his fingertips. He felt dizzy, like he was going to collapse. And just as he was about to topple to the tile floor, the roots around his tongue vanished, and the trees in his mouth melted to licorice.

Horace sighed with relief, then burped and felt a round object come up from his stomach to his throat and into his mouth.

Horace took a ball off his tongue and held it in his palm. It looked like a large orange seed, but was shiny like a marble.

Bwoop—bwoop—bwoop! the alarm kept screaming. Fire-truck sirens grew louder and louder. Was the school really on fire? If so, Horace knew he'd better get out of there fast. He wasn't sure what superpowers the cupcakes would give him, but he didn't think they'd make him fireproof.

He tucked the ball into his cape pocket, then reached for the red cupcake and stuffed it in his mouth.

This cake was so spongy, Horace had a hard time tearing it with his teeth. No matter how hard and fast he chewed, he couldn't break it into pieces small enough to swallow. And the sharp tips of the blue wings kept poking him in the gums.

Not to mention the taste.

If Horace had thought he was a good baker because of how delicious the orange cupcake was, now he thought he was the worst cupcake maker in the world. He had never tasted anything so awful. Even Snoodles and Cheaze didn't taste this bad. Horace had never eaten a bicycle tire with sour cherry sauce before, but if he had, he was sure this was exactly how it would have tasted.

He kept chewing and chewing and looking in the mirror to see what was happening in his mouth. The cake wouldn't be torn, and just as he was about to spit it into a toilet, the hundreds of little wings began flapping. They beat faster and faster until they flew off the cupcake and soared around Horace's mouth, breaking the cake into tiny pieces and pushing it down his throat. When they were done with the cupcake, they beat against his lips. They forced him to open his mouth as wide as he could, then flew out in a V formation and soared out the bathroom window.

It was one of the weirdest things Horace had ever seen.

The fire alarm suddenly stopped blaring. The red light stopped flashing. "False alarm. Everyone may return to their classes," Principal Nosair announced over the loudspeaker. "It appears that two of our students pulled the alarm as a prank. And I'm sorry to say those two students are Auggie and Xax Blootin. They will certainly be punished for such wrongdoing."

Horace gasped. Xax and Auggie would never pull the fire alarm unless there really was a fire. He hid his backpack behind the toilet and walked to the door. As he reached to pull the door open, the fingers of his right hand began wiggling in every direction so fast he couldn't get them to turn the doorknob. Then when he reached to open the door with his left hand, all those fingers began to wiggle uncontrollably. Horace stood back and looked at himself in the bathroom mirror. The wiggles crept from his fingers to his arms to his body, neck, legs, and head until he was twisting and spinning, buck-

ing and flailing, jibbing and gyrating in every
direction like each part of his body was a sepa-
rate tornado spinning every which way.

Horace grew dizzier and dizzier. His stomach felt like a cement mixer filled with Snoodles
and Cheaze. He was spinning and twisting as
fast as water in a flushed toilet, so completely
out of control he thought he'd never stop.

And then he blacked out.

Chapter 13

UP AND STUCK

Horace woke to find himself tangled in the town flag that hung on a tall pole in front of the school. His legs were wrapped around the bright white cloth, and his arms clutched the picture of the town mascot: a pink dodo bird.

Horace held on as tight as he could. How in the world did he end up there? How in the world would he get down?

He looked down at the school yard. The last of the kids were returning to the school after the false fire alarm. The fire truck was already driving back across town to the station house.

And then Horace saw them.

Gathered far across the playground and hiding behind some bushes were the twenty second-grade Lily Deaver girls, carrying their fake Lily Deaver totes. Each girl held an orange Chef Nibbles phone in her hand.

Somehow Nibbles must have gotten Auggie and Xax to pull the alarm so the second-graders could escape their classroom.

Horace heard a voice coming from the front of the school. Principal Nosair and Chef Nibbles were leading Xax and Auggie down the front steps. The boys stared straight ahead and looked as if they didn't even know what was going on. They walked as if they were sleepwalking.

"Thank you for taking the twins home," Principal Nosair told the chef. "I'm going to have a serious talk with Mayor and Mrs. Blootin about the boys' behavior."

"Don't worry," Chef Nibbles told the principal. "I'm very good friends with Mayor Blootin. I'll take the boys directly home." He opened the back door of his van, lifted in Xax and Auggie, then slammed the door shut.

Chef Nibbles reached into his coat and took out his bright orange cell phone. "I'll phone their father right now to let him know," he said.

"Thanks for your help discovering who set off the alarm," Principal Nosair told him. "And thanks for delivering all the Snoodles and Cheaze." The principal shook Chef Nibbles' hand, then walked back into the school.

Horace looked from the van to the Lily Deaver girls across the school yard. He had a bad feeling Chef Nibbles wasn't taking Xax and Auggie home. How could he rescue Auggie and Xax from Chef Nibbles when he also had to stop the Lily Deaver Scouts?

Horace watched as Chef Nibbles looked at his watch.

Bong. The bell in the Town Hall tower struck one o'clock.

Horace knew that if he had any powers, he needed to know now. He released the flag with one hand and pointed his fingers.

Nothing happened. He didn't fly. And his fingertips didn't grow metal scoops.

Horace took a deep breath and blew as hard as he could.

Nope, no fire.

He wrapped a hand around the pole and tried to bend it in half.

It wouldn't budge. Nope, no super strength.

He bent an elbow and a knee.

Nope, no lightning bolts.

And he wasn't becoming flat as a piece of paper so he could float to the ground.

Weren't the cupcakes he made good for anything?

Chef Nibbles flipped open his phone. "Speed-dial all second-grade Lily Deaver Scouts," he told the phone. Across the yard, the twenty Lily Deaver girls stood at attention, flipped open their phones, and listened.

Chef Nibbles spoke into his phone: "Scouts, commence the gravy-nating of Blootinville." He snapped the phone closed, climbed into the van, and drove out of the parking lot with Xax and Auggie in the back.

The Lily Deaver Scouts immediately broke into ten pairs and ran out of the school yard to spread across town.

Whether he had superpowers or not, Horace knew he had to get down from the flagpole as fast as he could. Auggie and Xax had to be saved from Chef Nibbles, and the town had to be saved from the Lily Deaver Scouts. Horace wrapped both his arms around the pole and reached over with his legs so he'd be able to slide to the ground.

But just then, from out of the ground at the bottom of the flagpole, a set of sharp claws appeared, and then the head of a porcupine.

Prickles! The neighbor's pet porcupine who had eaten Melody's cupcakes! Obviously the powers lasted a lot, lot longer in animals than they did in ten-year-old boys.

Prickles blew a burst of fire into the air, then jabbed his super-strength claws into the flagpole, splitting it in two. Horace suddenly found himself crashing to the ground.

Chapter 14

FOLLOW THE BOUNCING BOY

Yowee-zowee-zooks!" Horace cried.

There was the ground, there was Horace, and there was nothing in between to catch him.

Scared by the sight of the falling superhero, Prickles scrambled back into his hole and burrowed out of sight.

Was this another punishment for not listening to his sister's warning about trying the cupcakes without her? And why did the powers last so long in Prickles? Was it because the smaller you were, the longer they lasted?

Horace shut his eyes and waited for the moment when his body would strike the ground. It would only be a matter of seconds.

One . . . two . . .

Boing.

Instead of feeling his body hit the pavement and crunch into a million bits, Horace felt his body bend, then . . . *bounce.*

He opened his eyes. He was soaring high in the air, even higher than the school. He'd bounced off the ground like a Super Ball!

And then his body began falling again. This time, when he hit the ground, he bent his legs and sprang forward. His body shot skyward, bouncing out of the school yard and all the way down the street. He finally landed smack-dab in front of the Food-to-Eat Super-Duper Market and grabbed hold of a lamppost so he wouldn't bounce back into the air again.

Horace stood and listened. From inside the market, he heard screams. The electric doors opened, and a crowd of people rushed out dripping with thick, brown, goopy gravy. It slid down their faces and stuck to their clothes.

"Look what those terrible Lily Deaver girls have done!" a woman shouted.

"They're monsters! They should be arrested!" a man shrieked.

"That Lily Deaver is a witch!" a lady screamed as gravy dripped down her nose.

A little girl with a glop of gravy covering her face pointed at Horace. "Mommee! He's here! It's the Cupcaked Crusader! He'll save us!"

The crowd turned to Horace.

"You can save us, can't you?!"

"You must stop Lily Deaver and her girls!"

"Save our town, Cupcaked Crusader!"

Horace felt the tip of his nose itch, but he ignored it. "Don't worry. I'll take care of this immediately," he said in a calm voice. He turned and marched toward the door of the market. His nose grew itchier and itchier. Why was it itching so much? As he passed through the sliding doors, the store manager rushed to him.

She stood in front of Horace and knelt on the floor. "Please help us. Two Lily Deaver girls have ruined half the market, and nothing will stop them."

"I'll take care of it straightaway," Horace replied. He twitched his nose to stop it from itching, but as he did, it exploded with an orange mist that completely covered the store manager, sealing her in a see-through orange shell.

"Oops, excuse me," he said, then he stuck out

his tongue and gave the shell a poke with its tip.

It was candy! His second power was that he could twitch his nose and freeze people in an orange candy coating.

Cupcaked-Crusader-Incredible!

The candy-coated woman screamed from inside the shell. She was not nearly as excited about Horace's new power as he was, so he instantly pounded on the coating with a fist. The shell cracked and shattered to the floor like a pile of broken glass. "There you go," Horace told her. "Sorry about that. Sometimes I forget my powers." He pointed to the candy on the floor. "Take a bite. It tastes pretty good."

KABLAMMO–WHAMMO–BAMMO!

A wave of gravy exploded over the supermarket, covering the bakery, deli counter, and salad bar. Horace ran over to see two Nibblettes running down the frozen-food aisle. The girls pulled the lids of their snack cans, then tossed them at the freezers. Some customers were so covered with gravy that they were stuck to the floor.

The two girls laughed like wild hyenas and reached into their bags for more snack cups.

The Cupcaked Crusader would put a stop to this.

Horace jumped on the floor, bounced to the ceiling, and landed in front of the girls, grabbing hold of a shelf to keep from bouncing again. "Release those snack cups," he commanded.

"Who are you?" one of the girls sneered.

"You're just a purple runt," the other jeered.

"I'm the Cupcaked Crusader," Horace said. He gave two twitches of his nose, and orange fog blew out of his nostrils. It covered the two girls and froze them in a candy coating.

"That will hold them for a while," Horace told the store manager on his way out. "But now I've got to save the rest of the town." He took a jump and bounced away as people cheered.

• • •

Horace bounced through town, spotting more and more of the Nibblettes destroying restaurants, food stands, bakeries, and snack bars.

At the Crumbly-Tooth Candy Shop & Dentist Office, Horace froze two of the scouts in the orange candy coating before they could toss their snack cups at a display of chocolate-covered celernips.

At the Eat like an Animal Restaurant & Slop Bin, two Nibblettes had already gravy-nated a busload of Russian tourists while they were busy eating from a cow trough. Horace froze the girls before they could gravy-nate an old man and woman who were pecking seeds out of bird feeders.

Horace bounced from restaurant to restaurant and store to store, twitching his nose and coating each Nibblette with a hard orange candy shell. Sometimes he found the girls had destroyed part of the store, and sometimes they'd already destroyed it all. Poor Mr. Howlly would have to completely rebuild his doughnut shop. Of course, first he'd have to get unstuck from the huge glop of gravy that covered him from

neck to feet. With the gravy covering him and his loud wailing, Mr. Howlly really did look and sound exactly like a walrus.

After an hour of jumping, leaping, and bouncing around town, Horace had successfully stopped eighteen of the twenty Nibblettes. The only two he couldn't find were his sister and her best friend Betsy Roach. He searched the Cheese Doodle Emporium, the Marshmallow Den, and Señorita Paperelli's Pizza-Making

Monkey Restaurant, then decided he'd better head over to the Nibbles factory and rescue Xax and Auggie.

Horace bounced four giant bounces, passing through several neighborhoods where people cheered.

"Save our town!" a woman shouted from atop her roof.

"You're my hero!" Sara Willow called from her bedroom window.

Horace blushed. *He* was Sara Willow's hero...

As long as he wore a costume and had super-powers.

But Horace couldn't think about that now.

He took one-two-three more bounces and found himself at the door to Chef Nibbles' factory.

Chapter 15

SNOODLEBOUND

Horace took a jump and bounced up to an open window at the top of the building. He grabbed hold of the windowsill, pulled himself up, and sat on its ledge. One hundred feet below, the factory floor bustled with activity. Pots were steaming and bubbling with Snoodles and Cheaze. Dozens of workers in bright orange jumpsuits dashed about, filling and labeling cans, packing boxes, and loading them onto trucks.

Chef Nibbles stood on a stage in the middle of the room and barked. "Fill—Fill—Fill! Box—Box—Box! Load—Load—Load!" he yelled through a megaphone. The workers scurried about, doing exactly what they were told.

Finally, all the trucks were completely loaded, and Chef Nibbles barked one final command. "Take my Snoodles and Cheaze all around Blootinville and don't come back until every can has been sold!"

The employees jumped into their trucks and sped away, leaving Chef Nibbles standing alone on the stage listening to the humming machinery. He stepped down from the stage and went to a door at the side of the room and opened it. "Come on out," he barked.

Out shuffled Auggie and Xax. They were bound back-to-back with thick ropes of Snoodles. Nibbles pulled on Xax's nose, leading the boys into the room.

"Yowch!" Xax cried.

"You better let us go," Auggie said. "We'll tell our dad you hypnotized us to make us into zombies, and then you'll go to jail forever."

Chef Nibbles laughed and held up two orange cell phones. "The spell I put on you at lunch may have worn off, but after I hypnotize you again and tell you to only use my special cell phones, all I'll have to do is call you and, at the sound of my voice, you'll be my slaves just like the Lily Deaver girls." He tucked the phones into his pocket then took out a long sparkly gold Snoodle strand and waved it before Xax's eyes. "Follow the wiggling Snoodle," he instructed.

"Don't look at it, Xax!" Auggie shouted.

"Isn't it a beautiful Snoodle?" Chef Nibbles asked.

Xax shut his eyes. "I won't! I won't."

The Cupcaked Crusader had seen enough. Horace leaped to the floor and landed right beside Chef Nibbles, grabbing hold of a large pot so he wouldn't bounce back up in the air. "The jig's up, Nibbles. Surrender now," he commanded, just like he remembered a TV cop saying. He grabbed the Snoodle from Nibbles, took a jump, and bounced high into the air, tossing the Snoodle as hard as he could.

Kersplat!

It stuck to the ceiling.

The chef spun around. "Who is that? What's going on?" he asked.

"The Cupcaked Crusader!" Xax shouted.

"We knew you'd come and save us!" Auggie exclaimed.

Horace bounced to the floor and stood in front of Chef Nibbles. "It's time to put a stop to you, Nibbles. I've frozen almost all your Nibblettes, and now it's your turn." He twitched his nose.

Nothing happened.

Horace twitched it again.

Nothing. He must have used up all the powers freezing the girls.

Whoops. Now what?

Nibbles smiled. "You think you can stop me with a nose twitch? I don't think so. Bye-bye, superhero. I have to round up my girls." He kicked Horace in the knee. Horace fell to the ground, and the chef ran out of the factory. As Horace got to his feet, he could hear him driving away.

"Are you guys okay?" Horace asked.

"We're all right," Auggie said. "But you've got to stop him."

"How do I know where he's going?" Horace asked.

"The map on the wall," Auggie answered. "All the orange lights show where the Lily Deaver girls are. It tracks them by their cell phones."

Horace ran over to the map and saw blinking orange lights at the nine places he'd stopped Lily Deaver girls. Then he saw two flashing lights at a place where he hadn't been yet. He immediately knew where he'd find his sister and her friend. "Okay, guys, I'm off to save the town. See you later."

Xax stomped his foot. "Hey, free us first."

"Don't let him come back and make us Nibblettes," Auggie said.

"Oh yeah. Sorry," Horace said. "I haven't been a superhero for very long, so sometimes I forget how it works." He ran back to the twins and tugged on the Snoodles. They were tied too tight. There was only one way to break them. Horace opened his mouth and chewed through the Snoodles until they lay in a pile on the floor.

Xax and Auggie were freed.

"Thanks, Horace," Xax said.

"No problem," Horace replied, spitting a bite of Snoodles onto the factory floor.

"Now go get Nibbles," Auggie said.

Horace nodded, bounced through the open window, and out into the sky.

Next stop: the Deviled Egg Cafe.

Chapter 16

THE LAST OF THE NIBBLETTES

Bouncing across town, Horace saw a trail of destruction that he knew would lead directly to his sister. The Laughing Cow Steak House, the Tummyache Bakery, and the International House of Gummy had windows and doors overflowing with gravy. A Chef Nibbles truck was parked on every corner, waiting for all the food shops to be ruined so people would have to buy cans of Snoodles and Cheaze for dinner.

Horace landed in front of the Deviled Egg Café. It was shaped just like an egg, with a door at the tip and a yellow slide leading out like a broken yolk. Melody and Betsy Roach were staring into the windows and reached into their tote bags for the snack cups. Horace ran to the girls and grabbed their arms. "Stop in the name of the law," he ordered.

Betsy tried to pull away. "You're not a policeman," she said. "You're just a dopey superhero."

Melody stared at her brother. "What kind of ridiculous creature are you?" she asked.

Horace leaned to her ear and whispered, "I'm Horace. Remember? You made me this Cupcaked Crusader costume. Chef Nibbles hypnotized you and your friends with his cell phones and made you zombies so you'd destroy the town."

Melody turned up her nose. "I don't remember anything about anything. All I know is that if I want to be a good Nibblette, I must follow my leader's orders." She turned to Betsy. "Swat him," she instructed. The girls lifted their tote bags and began batting Horace over the head.

Horace released them, covering his head with his hands and backing away.

"Quick, immobilize him," Melody said. Betsy and Melody withdrew two snack cups. "Prepare

to pull the lid," Melody told her friend. "Ready, aim—"

The girls pulled the lids.

Horace bounced into the sky above the girls' heads.

The girls took aim and hurled the snack packs high above their heads at Horace.

But not high enough. The snack packs exploded in the air, missing Horace and showering the gravy back down on them. The goop coated the girls' faces and soaked their bodies so they couldn't move their arms or legs.

Horace landed on the ground, smiling at his good work. The last of the Nibblettes had been stopped.

Screech!

Chef Nibbles' van pulled into the restaurant parking lot. He leaned out the window with a nasty grin. "So, Cupcaked Crusader, you think you can put a stop to me just because you captured my Nibblettes?" he asked. "Well, I'll get away from Blootinville for now, but I'll be back someday, and then I'll take over the whole town."

But just as the chef was about to drive off, a hole suddenly appeared by the van's back tire, then two sets of claws, and then the head of Prickles the porcupine. The animal snapped its mouth open and closed as if he were hungry.

"Prickles, attack!" Horace called.

Nibbles took his foot off the brake to drive away, but before he could pull out, the porcupine exhaled a blast of fire, melting the two back tires to the pavement.

"I don't think your van's going anywhere." Horace laughed.

Prickles burrowed out of his hole, pointed his paws, and flew far off into the sky. Horace let out a loud laugh. He bet Melody had never thought her cupcakes would make a porcupine into a superhero!

Nibbles frowned and leaped from the van. "My two feet will do just fine," he said, sneering. He began running as fast as he could.

Horace leaped to bounce and follow, but nothing happened. He only jumped a few inches off the ground before landing. The power had worn off, and Nibbles was getting farther and farther away.

And then Horace remembered.

The orange ball from the cupcake! It had to have some powers that might help.

He quickly reached into his wing pocket and took out the small ball. Should he eat it or throw it?

Horace wasn't sure what the ball would do, but he did know that this was his last chance to stop the chef. He took the ball in his hand and threw it at the villain as hard as he could.

The ball sailed through the air, flying high in

the sky, then dipping lower and lower until—

Bull's-eye!

It cracked against Chef Nibbles' head, pouring an orange fog all over him.

Horace couldn't see through the orange cloud. He ran closer—but not too close—and observed. A giant orange bubble slowly rose out of the orange cloud. And inside the bubble stood Chef Nibbles. "Get me out of here!" he screamed. He was banging his hands and stomping his feet against the bubble's sides, but it was no use. The bubble wouldn't burst. It rose higher and higher, drifting farther and farther away, until a wind blew, lifting the bubble beyond Rumbly Mountain and out of Blootinville.

Horace took a deep breath. Mission accomplished. With luck, the bubble would take Nibbles far enough away from Blootinville so that he'd never come back.

But if he did, next time Horace knew he'd be ready for him now that he knew how to bake his own cupcakes.

Chapter 17

MELODY SMELODY

BLOOTINVILLE BANNER MORNING EDITION
**CUPCAKED CRUSADER BUBBLES NIBBLES**

by Mari Splattly

The town of Blootinville breathed a great sigh of relief after the Cupcaked Crusader saved it from a permanent diet of Snoodles and Cheaze. Not only did the half-pint-sized superhero trap Chef Nibbles in a huge bubble cage and send him floating out of town, but he also saved the second-grade Lily Deaver troop and Mayor Blootin's twin sons from becoming Nibbles' zombies for the rest of their lives.

Although the Cupcaked Crusader stopped Nibbles before he could destroy all the food markets and restaurants in Blootinville, many shops did suffer physical damage as a result of the many gravy snack cups thrown by the Lily Deaver Scouts. While zombies, the girls claimed that Ms. Lily Deaver had ordered them to destroy the food shops in town. This was obviously not true.

"Lily Deaver has always been my hero," Melody Splattly cried into her Lily Deaver handkerchief. "I hope she won't kick me out of her troop because I did this. I never ever really wanted to be a Nibblette."

Ms. Lily Deaver appeared on Blootinvision TV early yesterday evening and announced that the girls were forgiven for their actions. "Sometimes even a Lily Deaver Scout can be tricked into doing the wrong thing. But usually only once," Lily Deaver said.

Each of the Lily Deaver girls handed her Chef Nibbles cell phone over to the police so it could be destroyed.

And what will become of the thousands of cans of Snoodles and Cheaze? In a surprise twist, when Mr. Tweetotter overheated a pan on his stove last night, he discovered that if a Snoodles and Cheaze casserole is baked at 500 degrees, it becomes as hard as a brick. Tweetotter plans on baking hundreds of Snoodles and Cheaze bricks and using them to build an All-You-Can-Eat Hot Dog Castle.

Gravy cleanup began yesterday evening after the police stormed Chef Nibbles' abandoned factory and found the formula for the mixture that melts the horrendously gooey gravy. According to the police, to remove gravy from buildings, hair, clothes, or skin, mix a quart of vinegar, four chopped onions, and a gallon of barbecue sauce in a bathtub, then scrub it into whatever needs cleaning. The gravy will wash away instantly. Unfortunately, the smell from the vinegar, onions, and barbecue sauce will linger for three additional days.

And if anyone knows the whereabouts of Prickles the porcupine, please phone Mr. and Mrs. Honker. He was last scene flying in the sky high above the Deviled Egg Cafe.

The next day Horace and Melody walked to school. Horace wore his usual jeans and T-shirt. Melody wore a clean, newly ironed lavender Lily Deaver outfit and matching sash, stockings, shoes, headband, and gloves.

Horace raised his nose in the air and took a sniff. "Hmm ... what *is* that splendiferous smell. It stinks like lavender Lily Deaver perfume mixed with vinegar, onions, and barbecue sauce." He laughed quietly and took a little hop.

Melody pouted. "Can you still smell it?" she asked. "I thought I put on enough perfume so you couldn't."

Horace wrinkled his nose and took another sniff. "Yup, you're still a stinky Nibblette," he answered with a laugh.

"It's not funny," Melody fumed. "Don't call me that."

They walked down the hill and approached the school. "You're just lucky I was smart enough to bake the cupcakes and save the town," Horace said.

Melody wrinkled her mouth. "Maybe so, but I'll *never* give up my Lily Deaver equipment

again. Which means *I'm* back in charge, and *you'll* never have any cupcakes without me baking them."

Horace turned away from his sister and ran up the front steps of the school. "You could at least thank me for saving you," he called over his shoulder. "And fix the hands of my costume so I don't have to wear mittens anymore."

Melody chased after her brother, grabbing his arm and stopping him by the front door. She lifted a hand and poked him on the top of his head with a finger. "*Thank you*, Horace," she said in a sweet voice, and then she leaned in close and whispered, "But if you *ever* touch my Lily Deaver things again, I'll feed you cupcakes that make you shrink to half your size forever." And then she pranced through the school doors and off to her classroom.

Horace frowned and stepped into the school.

"Hey, triplet!" Auggie and Xax called. The twins ran over to their friend. Auggie waved the newspaper article. "We read all about it this morning," he said in a hushed voice.

"You're even more famous than before," Xax said quietly. "It's going to be—"

But before Xax could finish his sentence, Horace's attention was drawn to a special someone entering the school.

Sara Willow walked by with her hair sprayed pink and combed into the shape of a cupcake. She smiled at the boys. "I did my hair like this in honor of the Cupcaked Crusader," she said.

Horace's eyes went wide with excitement. "Just for me!" he shouted. "Gee, thanks!"

Sara scowled. "I did my hair special for *the Cupcaked Crusader*," she scoffed. "Why would I do it special for you?" She folded her arms across her chest and stomped down the hall.

Horace turned and leaned his forehead against the wall.

Xax patted his back. "Don't be upset. We know you're the hero who saved the day."

"Yeah, Horace," Auggie said. "If it wasn't for you, Chef Nibbles would have taken over the town."

Horace slowly turned his head away from

the wall and flashed a huge grin at his friends.

"Why are you smiling like a crazy jack-o'-lantern?" Auggie asked.

"We thought you were unhappy because Sara was mean to you," Xax said.

Horace laughed. "True, Sara was mean to me," he admitted. "But she *did* talk to me, didn't she? And before you know it, maybe we'll be friends. Don't you think so?"

"Oh, Horace," Xax said, shaking his head so his hair fell over his eyes.

"Oh, Horace," Auggie said, reaching a hand up to comb his bangs over the top of his head.

The three boys began walking down the hall to their classroom.

"So," Horace asked, "what conspiracy are we going to investigate today?"